Stella Dadzie

Stella is a feminist writer, historian and education activist, best known for her co-authorship of *Heart of the Race: Black Women's Lives in Britain* which was re-published by Verso in 2018 as a Feminist Classic. She is a founder member of Organisation of Women of African and Asian Descent (OWAAD), a national umbrella group for Black women that emerged in the late 1970s as part of the British Civil Rights movement.

She has written numerous publications and resources aimed at promoting good practice with Black learners and other minorities, including resources to decolonise and diversify the UK national curriculum in schools and colleges.

Her most recent book, *A Kick in the Belly: Women, Slavery and Resistance* (Verso, 2020) centres women in the story of West Indian enslavement. She also wrote the foreword to *Hairvolution: Her Hair, Her Story, Our History* (Supernova Books) in 2021.

First published in the UK in 2024 by Supernova Books, an imprint of Aurora Metro Publications Ltd. 80 Hill Rise, Richmond, TW10 6UB www.aurorametro.com info@aurorametro.com

X: @aurorametro F: facebook.com/AuroraMetroBooks

Printed by 4edge Ltd. Essex, UK on paper that has been sustainably resourced.

ISBNs: 978-1-913641-41-2 (print)   978-1-913641-40-5 (ebook)

Encounters with
James Baldwin

Celebrating 100 years

Introduced by
Stella Dadzie

Edited by
Kadija George Sesay
& Cheryl Robson

SUPERNOVA BOOKS

Kadija George Sesay is a Sierra Leonean/British scholar and activist. Her doctoral thesis on Black Publishers and Pan-Africanism will be published by Africa World Press. She is the Publications Manager for Inscribe/Peepal Tree Press, where she commissions anthologies, such as *Glimpse*, a Black British speculative fiction anthology. The first anthology she edited was *Six Plays by Black and Asian Women Writers* for Aurora Metro. Since then, she has edited several other anthologies and is publisher of *SABLE LitMag*.

She has published her own poetry, short stories and essays. Her latest work is in *New Daughters of Africa* and her solo poetry collection is *Irki*; her forthcoming collection is *The Modern Pan-Africanist's Journey.* She is founder of the first International Black Speculative Writing Festival, co-founder of Mboka Festival of Arts, Culture and Sport, and founder of the 'AfriPoeTree' app. She has judged several writing competitions and is the resident judge for the SI Leeds Literary Prize. She has received awards and fellowships for her work in the creative arts.

Cheryl Robson is the founder of award-winning independent publisher Aurora Metro, home to the popular culture imprint Supernova Books and the drama imprint Amber Lane Press. As publisher, Cheryl has been shortlisted for the ITV National Diversity Awards for both Lifetime Achievement and as an Entrepreneur. Aurora Metro has been shortlisted twice for the Independent Publisher Guild national awards for Diversity in Publishing.

Cheryl is also an award-winning playwright, editor and film-maker but is perhaps best-known for her successful campaign to commission and erect a bronze statue in honour of Virginia Woolf which was unveiled in Richmond in 2022 and has become a tourist attraction close to the publisher's offices and bookshop, Books on the Rise.

Contents

"The challenge is in the moment, the time is always now."

– **James Baldwin**

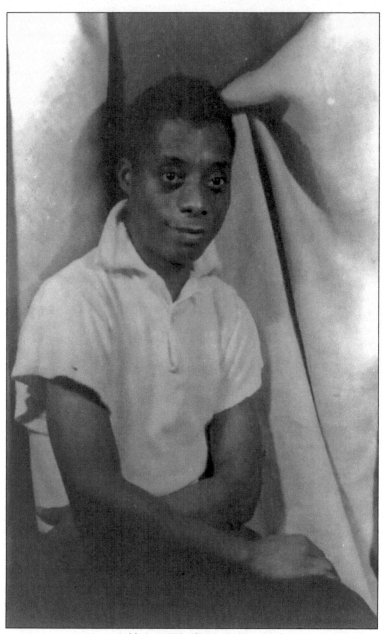
James Baldwin, 1955. Photo: Carl Van Vechten
Library of Congress

Introduction

Stella Dadzie

"Love takes off the masks we fear we cannot live without
and know we cannot live within."

– James Baldwin, *The Fire Next Time*

Despite the upheavals and injustices of the past century, mine
was a blessed generation. As young Black people, encountering
a world of entrenched racial injustice, our mentors included a
veritable roll call of inspirational African Americans – Malcolm
X, Martin Luther King Jr, Angela Davis, Maya Angelou, to
name but a few – women and men who point-blank refused
to accept a version of themselves that was anything less than
equal to those who would have them believe otherwise.

Amongst those visionaries was James Baldwin – a diminutive
man with a permanently crinkled brow and an infectious, gap-
toothed smile – whose writings went beyond an indictment
of racial oppression to confront issues of Black masculinity,
sexuality, and homophobia. He made no attempt to hide his
sexuality. In this respect, he was way ahead of his time. Long
before terms like 'intersectionality' and 'non-binary' entered
our common parlance, Baldwin recognised the complex
ambiguities that define our sexual identity. His vision was of
a world free of hatred, prejudice and division. His bequest to
future generations was a fierce abhorrence of injustice and an
equally fierce belief in the enduring power of love.

Born in Harlem, New York, in 1924, James Arthur Baldwin
(né Jones) grew up in a home where his birth-father remained

absent and unnamed. His mother, Emma, had joined the swelling ranks of Southern hopefuls who had fled north in a bid to escape poverty and segregation. The man she subsequently married, an embittered labourer and fiery Baptist preacher, was old enough to be her father. Like Baldwin's paternal grandfather, he may well have been born into slavery.

James Baldwin's relationship with his stepfather proved turbulent. Drawn to books and writing from an early age, he refused to accept the idea that his love of reading and films, and the fact that he had white school friends, was a road to damnation. With the encouragement of his mother and the support of teachers who recognised his early talent, Baldwin spent many hours in the public library on 135th Street, immersed in the novels of Dickens, Dostoyevsky, and Harriet Beecher Stowe. He wrote prolifically, almost as soon as he could hold a pen. By the time he entered his teens, he had already published a number of short stories and poems in his school magazine. He had also followed in his stepfather's footsteps, becoming a youth minister in a local Pentecostal church at the age of fourteen.

As a young Black man growing up in Harlem in the 1940s, Baldwin encountered the harsh realities of racism on a daily basis, from casual discrimination and deferred aspirations to the poverty and violence of life in the ghetto. On leaving school, with his widowed mother and eight younger siblings to help support, college would become a distant dream. Instead, he worked in a variety of low-paid jobs whilst continuing to write.

Raised to believe that homosexuality was a carnal sin, it is no surprise that Baldwin struggled with his sexual orientation throughout his teens. Despite several relationships with women, he knew he was attracted to men. Moving from Harlem to the more liberal environment of Greenwich Village freed him from the constraints of his religious upbringing, empowering him to own his identity as a gay man. But as an aspiring writer and the grandson of an enslaved and vilified people, he had other identities to grapple with. He also longed to escape the restrictions imposed by his race and class.

In 1945, with help from the novelist Richard Wright, he won a fellowship, allowing him to devote more time to his writing. Soon, his essays and short stories began to appear in national publications. His decision to move to Paris three years later, thanks to another fellowship, proved life-changing. Away from the claustrophobic confines of post-war America, where segregation and racial hurdles intruded into every aspect of his existence, he was finally able to complete his first novel. As he later remarked, "once I found myself on the other side of the ocean, I could see where I came from very clearly."[1]

The result was *Go Tell It on the Mountain*, a semi-autobiographical novel published in 1953, which explored the father-son relationship and the complexities of spiritual redemption. He saw the book as his way of confronting the issues that had caused him the most hurt, so he could move on to explore other themes. His second novel, *Giovanni's Room*, published in 1956, was a bold attempt to do just that. Centred on the life of a white American man living in France who struggles with his homosexuality and tries without success to conceal it, it was dedicated to Baldwin's former lover whom he had lived with in Switzerland, who had chosen, finally, to marry a woman. A story about pain, truth, regret and redemption, it was destined to become a classic gay text.

Baldwin was at his most eloquent when speaking out about race in America. In *Notes of a Native Son*, published in 1955, he explores the complexities of Black life through a pre-Civil Rights lens, commenting wryly on the casual racism African Americans encounter throughout their lives. No topic escapes his critical gaze – literature, the theatre, the Black press, the Black church, his relationship with his

---

1 James Baldwin Reflects on 'Go Tell It' PBS Film, by Leslie Bennetts, *New York Times,* Jan 10th 1985.

stepfather, his experiences of being denied entry to segregated venues, and his observations of what it meant to be a Black man living in post-war France. His insights resonate to this day. Seventy years ago, Baldwin was calling out colourism, stereotyping, anti-Semitism, tokenism, press sensationalism, church hypocrisy, racism in the military and the alienation of immigrants – issues that remain as relevant now as they ever were, as the contributions in this book will confirm.

A decade later, at the height of the struggle for Civil Rights, he resumed his critique in *The Fire Next Time* (1963), exploring the interface between racism, power and identity in two powerfully argued essays. The first, written as a letter to his nephew, urges future generations of young Black people not to let racism define who they are or what they can become. The second, delivered with the fiery eloquence of a sermon, addresses Americans in general, presenting an indictment of the country's institutions, particularly the hypocrisy of the Black church, and calling for a new moral sensibility. As David McAlmont states in his review of Raoul Peck's film about Baldwin, *I Am Not Your Negro*, he was "a necessary fly in [America's] illusionistic ointment."[2]

Baldwin was expounding critical race theory before we even gave it a name. It is no coincidence that those who seek to stifle such debates in our contemporary moment have included this book on their list of banned texts in North American schools. Nor should it surprise us, in these dystopian, truth-twisting times, that the very arguments he used in his plea for racial harmony – a more honest assessment of history, for example, or an end to racial oppression – are blamed for promoting division and intolerance. As Ewuare X. Osayande puts so eloquently in his poem 'Fahrenheit 1492', the allies of white supremacy have "Elvis Presleyed history" and seek to "gaslight the whole world".

---

2 https://www.huffingtonpost.co.uk/david-mcalmont/to-james-baldwin-on-the-o_b_15508928.html

Introduction

Baldwin had returned to America in 1957, on the cusp of the Civil Rights movement. He threw himself into the fray, touring the Southern States, marching in Selma and on Washington, speaking at rallies and meetings both at home and abroad. Black communities were his primary audience. As Tony Warner recalls in his essay 'James Baldwin and Black British Civil Rights', despite his growing international stature, in 1985, he even gave a speech at a public library in Hackney. His friendships and acquaintances included men from across the Black liberation spectrum – Malcolm X, Martin Luther King Jr, Medgar Evers, Louis Farrakhan – but he was never anyone's disciple.

His independent mind and eclectic range of interests were evidenced in a subsequent collection of essays, *Nobody Knows my Name* (1961) and in his third novel *Another Country* (1962). They move beyond issues of race and inter-racial relationships to explore themes such as bisexuality, domestic abuse, mental health, alienation and self-hatred. Human relationships in all their complexity were his muse, but race was always central to his discourse. As one biographer commented, "the whole racial situation, according to (this) novel, was basically a failure of love."[3]

Baldwin continued to write about race throughout his life. In his play *Blues for Mister Charlie* (1964) he confronts his audience with the exoneration of those who murdered Emmett Till, a teenage boy who was lynched for speaking to a white woman. Paterson Joseph describes his experience of acting in the play in his essay 'The Inspirational Blues' as a moment of epiphany, allowing him and his generation "to feel their sense of belonging as a casual, obvious and observable, quantifiable, and undeniable truth."

In Baldwin's short story collection, *Going to Meet the Man* (1965) he dissects racism in all its guises. Yet race is always explored through the prism of love, human frailty and what would nowadays be called intersectionality – what Alan Bell refers to in

---

3 *James Baldwin: Artist on Fire*, by W.J. Weatherby, New York: Dell, 1989.

'A Picture is Worth a Thousand Phone Calls' as "the complexities of navigating multiple identities." Queer themes loom large in Baldwin's work, and several of his fictional characters are, like him, either gay or bisexual. Despite the homophobia he encountered, particularly from Black Nationalists, as with his views about race and religion, he was never prepared to be silenced.[4]

In later life, he went on to lecture at a number of American universities. He also wrote several more novels, including *Tell Me How Long the Train's Been Gone* (1968), *If Beale Street Could Talk* (1974) which Barry Jenkins made into an Oscar-winning movie in 2018, *Just Above My Head* (1979) and his unfinished memoir, *Remembering This House*, written that same year, in which he uses the murders of Malcolm X, Martin Luther King and Medgar Evers, all men he thought of as friends, to explore America's contradictions, both past and present. As he continued to navigate the challenges of a white, male publishing world, Baldwin faced rejection from publishers, who claimed he was out of touch with contemporary America. He also faced growing rejection from some of his fellow Civil Rights activists, who deemed him to be too placatory. He was always a brilliant writer, determined to speak his truth and shame the devil (although not without a personal toll). And he was always a brutally honest thinker, who refused to jump on bandwagons simply because they rolled with the times.

Those grainy YouTube videos of Baldwin doing battle with the right-wing writer William F. Buckley at the Cambridge Union in 1965,[5] or firing off his salvos on the Dick Cavett[6] show in 1969, confirm that he was a wise, courageous, articulate man who had no qualms about speaking truth to power.[7] He was also a mesmerising speaker whose oratory skills were honed

4 see Eldridge Cleaver, *Soul on Ice*, in *Ramparts*, California, 1968 p.103.
5 Cambridge Union debate: https://www.youtube.com/watch?v=5Tek9h3a5wQ
6 Dick Cavett interview 1969: https://www.youtube.com/watch?v=WWwOi17WHpE

in the pulpit at an early age. Sixty years on, listening to Baldwin speak is like listening to an inspired, eloquent preacher, only the focus of his sermon is a different kind of religion – a religion informed by his unwavering belief in his people's rights to freedom and autonomy, expressed in a fervent prayer for the future of all humanity, Black or white, gay or straight. As Sonia Grant puts it in her essay, 'Can I get an Amen, Somebody?' his was a prophetic voice with no expiry date.

It should come as no surprise that Baldwin has had such a powerful and enduring legacy or that, nearly four decades after his death in France in 1987, he continues to influence our thinking in so many complex ways. Echoes of his voice can be heard in our poetry, our plays, our fiction, in our on-going narratives about race, class, gender and intersectionality. Sometimes we recognise the echo, sometimes we barely realise it's there but, as Zita Holbourne demonstrates in her poem 'What Kind of World is This?', it is as pervasive as the sentiments he expounded. In his essay 'Wherefore, Nuncle?' Tade Thompson says Baldwin gave him "permission to disagree, permission to think, and permission to have my own rage." SuAndi puts it another way in her essay 'For Jimmy,' crediting Baldwin with helping her to see the world she lives in "with different eyes." For Nducu wa Ngugi, whose essay 'The Fire is Now' references Baldwin's own essay 'The Fire Next Time', it's about the fact that he challenges us "to understand this world and [our] participation in it." Ronnie McGrath makes a similar observation in his essay, 'What's Love Got to do with it?': "He […] allowed me to see the profound beauty of being Black," he says, "and how to walk with my head held high in an often-hostile white world."

Similar insights are made or implied by every contributor. In her essay 'The Spirit of James Baldwin', Michelle Yaa Asantewa embodies him as the Yoruba deity Baba Esu, pointing out that he "opens the way for self-awareness and critical self-evaluation by vociferously challenging us to examine our lives, our humanity, and our struggles to survive." For Selina Brown, in her essay, 'Never Make Peace with Mediocrity' his words became a mantra, a constant reminder to refuse to settle for mediocrity, to "stand taller, to assert my worth, and to demand recognition for my capabilities."

In his essay, 'In a Photograph with James Baldwin', Fred D'Aguiar, who met 'Jimmy' in the flesh several months before he died, describes him as a man whose broad smile "rented all the space on his head", a man who "wrote as well as he talked", exuding wit, humour and confidence. Yet, perhaps our beloved Jimmy simply had a good front. His writings suggest that, behind that contagious smile of his, he grappled with numerous demons, many of which haunt us to this day.

Today, poverty, hunger, the workings of imperialism in Palestine, the Congo, and many other global arenas, continue to engage us. Michael McMillan sums it up neatly in his essay, 'Revisiting James Baldwin'. One of Baldwin's most enduring legacies, he says, was that he taught him to eschew "a happy smiling-face version of history, as if the past has no relevance to our dark present." We live in challenging times, with no room for the luxury of complacency. As Nii Ayikwei Parkes insists in his piece entitled 'Passing', "It's time to pass from comfort to radical alertness. It's Baldwin time."

The fascinating range of essays and poems in this book testify to a mindset, a way of seeing and being and engaging with life, particularly if you are young and Black. They will resonate deeply with readers who hanker for a different, more compassionate world. They are proof, if any were needed, that Baldwin's views have shaped and moulded the consciousness of generations of exiled Africans, not just in America but across the diaspora.

We stand on the shoulders of giants.

"Trust life, and it will teach you, in joy and sorrow, all you need to know."

– James Baldwin

Three Memories of Baldwin

Rashidah Ismaili AbuBakr

I was invited to Paule Marshall's apartment on Central Park, West and 100th Street which was the first time I met James Baldwin. I went to a party there with a Trinidadian named Dr. Wilfred Cartey. He was a poet and a critic and wrote one of the first major critiques of modern African literature called *Whispers of a Continent.* I don't even remember how we met, but Wilfred was one of those people who knew everybody, and everybody loved him. He was so charming, and everybody was just so amazed that he was so vibrant and alert and a ladies' man. Yet he was blind – how could he do this? A lot of men were envious of him. He was drop-dead gorgeous. About 6'1", or 6'2", very slender, with this absolutely velvet skin. And very arrogant. Because he knew he was gorgeous. He never used any help like a dog or a cane because he always had gorgeous women with him, and his family worshipped him and treated him like a king. So, I had the honour of being with him that evening when we went to Paule Marshall's apartment. Anyway, I had just read one of her books, *Brown Girl, Brownstones,* or *Selena,* so it was a big thing for me to go to her apartment. I hadn't moved to Harlem then; I was still living downtown in the early 1970s.

So we went there, and there was all this food and all these people, probably only about ten people, but it felt like more … you know how when you have a party that really is jamming, it was like that, that kind of energy. And everybody was comfortable and talking about politics and the latest this and the latest that. Between 10 and 11pm, the bell rings, and this little guy comes in, and like it's no big deal. Wilfred says, "Oh, hey, Jimmy." And he just goes off again.

Then this forever and ever woman comes in. And it's Miss Maya Angelou and she's wearing heels. She's about 6'3" in heels. And then there's Baldwin, who had come up before her on the elevator and she's cussing at him because he didn't hold the "so-so" door for her. And who does he think he is? And everybody's laughing. Oh, my, la-la-la. Before she walks in, she says, "Do you have my stuff?" And Paule runs to the bar and comes out with this bottle. Maya always preferred Johnny Walker. I don't remember if it was Red Label or Black Label, but it was one of those two.

Once she knew you had it, she was okay. And the party began. Everybody knew each other except me. And I meet this man and he shakes my hand. He had the most incredible eyes. He and Amiri Baraka had these what I call owl eyes. Very big, slightly protrusive, but invasive in the sense that they just sort of went into you. They really "saw you."

He looked at me and squeezed his eyes up and said, "How are you, my dear?"

Or something like that. Wilfred nudged me and I said, "I'm quite well, thank you. How are you?"

And he says, "Fair to middling."

I never forgot that because I didn't know that expression. And I thought, oh, I don't know how to answer that, so I better not say anything. But Wilfred knew me well and he explained it, "Rashidah, that means sometimes up and sometimes down."

I never forgot "fair to middling" after that. Then people started talking about literature and politics and the state of affairs. *Freedomways*[1] was active at that point. Baldwin was very involved in it. So, they would talk about the articles. It was not just stimulating, it was a really, very deep discussion of

---

1 *Freedomways* was the leading African American political and cultural journal of the 1960s. It launched in 1961 and ceased in 1985.

everything in a way that made you feel like you had to know all these things, that all of these things were important. Then out of all of that came a novel or a painting or a dance or an article. These were not just fluffy conversations.

All of a sudden, Maya would burst into song, and she would sing a blues and she would dance and kick up her long legs. Sometimes she and Louise Meriwether would banter because one could cuss as well as the other. I was very intimidated by Louise, but Maya wasn't intimidated by anybody. So that party was my first time meeting Baldwin.

His brother, David, bought a jazz club about two or three blocks away from where Paule lived. The spot was called 'Cedars' or 'Cellars' or something like that. And it was right off Amsterdam. Hugh Masekela used to play there. I mean, it was a really happening place.

Maya Angelou and James Baldwin had a very strong brother-sister relationship. They were like two naughty kids under the blanket talking about all of the adults in the room, snickering and laughing and poking fun. At the same time, they were very wise and insightful.

A lot of it was because of their experience. It could have been just the cultural difference between, say, growing up in Harlem or growing up in Arkansas where Maya was from. I was in my early twenties and in awe of everybody. Everyone seemed to be so sophisticated, intelligent, just always at the ready with a word or a phrase. So, I spent most of those times just looking and listening. And because they had long friendships, and they knew the people that they were talking about, they would make insider jokes about them and each other. They all had this kind of international worldliness about them that was alien to me.

Baldwin was a very caring person but he also had a mouth on him. He was not afraid to speak up. He was very bold and very unafraid to say anything. David, his brother, was almost always there to back him up. His fists were ready at the slightest hint of somebody disrespecting him; he was ready to pounce on them. So was Maya. They really were very protective of him. And then he would go away for long periods of time, I wouldn't see him.

All of those people were around the same age. They were all between two and three years apart. Louise Meriwether, died recently, about six months after her 100th birthday. So that whole crowd has gone now; everyone who was in that room, has physically gone, but me.

*

Another memory that I wanted to share is not so nice. There was a big to-do at a conference of major African writers that included Baldwin, Achebe, Bebey,[2] in 1980, in Gainesville, Florida. All the major writers were there. Baldwin was invited to speak as one of the keynote speakers. When he got to the microphone, it suddenly went dead. And then this voice comes over a loudspeaker and says, "Die, you f***ing, nigger, die... die... die." It was loud. And then it went blank, and then the microphone came back on.

Baldwin being Baldwin, handled it gracefully but it was a very big embarrassment. Baldwin came from that conference to us, at the African Literature Association conference in Florida. You could tell he was angry, really angry. And he was really hurt. He said, "I want to talk about this moment. What does it mean? And how do we respond to that?" Everybody was very upset that he was treated in such a way. A lot of the critics, especially the white critics, were complaining that he was writing the same novel over and over and over again. And I remember him saying, "If I wrote the same novel over and over again, I'd still be able to write the same novel the next day, because the same old s*** happens every day." That was his humour.

---

2 See the YouTube video 'James Baldwin Interrupted', https://www. youtube.com/watch?v=he7bx18yw34

He was almost in tears. I think that's one of my lasting images of him. He put himself out there. He put himself on the line to be a target and to show people how you go through that, how you work through that. But at the same time, he's a human being. So how do you not be bowed, but have your personhood be respected? No one ever found out who did it or how it happened. No other problems happened before and no other problems after. He said, "That was a statement. It was not an accident."

He was always very concerned about self-love. I think it pained him when people were deliberately mean and bullying. Those kinds of things really disturbed him and he understood what that means, to be a bully. He said the saddest thing was to be unlovable and he said that you feel unlovable because you don't love yourself. You have to be able to love yourself and that most people who don't love themselves can be very cruel to others.

Baldwin really loved people. He loved Black men. He loved Black women. He loved Black children. He loved Black adults, but he was very measured in his critique of people. He criticized the system, he criticized structures that oppressed and that kept people from realising their potential, but he didn't criticize somebody just because he was white, he criticised people who thought that they could do what they did because they were white. That's a very big difference. So, if you look at some of the comments that he makes about race, he talks a lot about love and being loving and being able to love. I think all that is quite philosophical. He was very Afrocentric in his thinking and his affiliation, I mean he was really, in his own way, a Pan-Africanist, too. He was a great writer and a great thinker, and a philosopher on love. Almost all of his work has a philosophical overtone to it.

*

Three Memories of Baldwin

This last memory I want to share is a much more pleasant one. My friend and I went to see Nina Simone at the Village Gate on Bleeker Street in the late 1970s or early 1980s.

There was a long queue with people saying she is ranting and raving, she's crazy, la la la and that was because the timing in between the last show and the upcoming show for which we had tickets was beginning to blend into one. She was on stage, but she was refusing to perform, because she said she wanted her money. A lot of mostly white people were saying, "Why do we put up with her? Who does she think she is?" And we didn't say anything. We went into the club, and it was full up to the rafters. When we finally got inside, the piano was on stage, but Nina was not. After maybe fifteen minutes or so she came out, everybody applauded, and she launched into what you could call a Nina Simone tirade. She was saying, "I am *not* a prima donna and it's not true what people are saying, all these things about me. I just want to be paid for my work. I am a musician, you know, I practise, I come to the performance. I'm ready to perform but I want my money. And I want to be paid for my work."

At first she was standing, and then finally she went and she sat at the piano. She started to play and then she stopped, and she said, "I'm not on the plantation anymore, I'm not your slave that you wind up and then I perform... I'm an artist." She laughed. She was really complaining about the treatment that the Village Gate had shown her. Then people started whispering and I see this figure coming in... I hadn't seen him for a very long time. But Baldwin, once you've seen him you can recognize him anywhere. So, I said to my friend, that looks like Jimmy Baldwin. He was going to take his seat and Nina Simone saw him and her whole body just changed... she almost jumped up. "Aha! There's my brother James Baldwin, now f*** with me if you want!" Everybody was clapping, somebody said something, so he went up and sat next to her at the piano and you could imagine him saying something like,

"Nina, what are you doing?" and he was trying to calm her down. He said, "You're a musician… just be a musician and do your job."

She said, "You stay right here," and he said something like, "You're testifying," or something like that. "Let's go to church." So, she started to play this song, "Take me to the water…" just some very simple chords and then Baldwin was singing with her. There were a lot of Black people in the audience and some of them knew the song and joined in.

The people's voices started to rise and suddenly we heard this wonderful voice from one of the Black women. She had closed her eyes and she was just singing with all her heart. Baldwin motioned for us to be quiet. You could hear her voice and it really calmed Nina down, and she just played and played, and the woman was just singing and after a while I guess the woman realised that she could only hear her own voice. Everybody was looking at her and just really loving it. And so, she got quieter and quieter and Baldwin motioned for her to continue singing to the end and then we all applauded. It was just a magical moment. I was blessed to be there at that time. Nina gave a two-hour non-stop performance that set.

It's one of those things, as they say – you had to be there.

Three Memories of Baldwin

Nina Simone and James Baldwin c. 1960s
Photo: New York Public Library

Blackspace

Victor Adebowale

The place between the listening and the heard

The seen and the looking

The want and the found

The sleep and the dream

Searching and the finding

We see ourselves in the mirrors of our own minds but what is between the image and the observer is reality unreflected in the physical

The question in the mind

Who

What

Is

That

Against the backdrop of experience

I can say my name on repeat, and it means

Nothing

As I awake in the morning and the information of life rushes in to fill the space of knowing

I am lost for an instant and I feel the fear of that space its possibility overwhelms, and I make my choice to tell the story given by what I see, hear, smell, relate, expect, understand.

I am safe

Blackspace

It is who I am now
Who your eyes set upon, and your history expects
I am your frightening other come to fill the space
To make your future in an instant
Address your ordinary fears now
I am the possible and the chance to change

Talking about Baldwin with Victor Adebowale

VICTOR: Let me say I'm not an expert on James Baldwin. No, no. I just fell in love with the guy (laughs).

CHERYL: Why did you fall in love with him?

VICTOR: I knew who James Baldwin was, but I'd not engaged with him until I went to the cinema to see the film *I'm Not Your Negro* in 2017. And it just blew me away. Baldwin's confidence, his sense of self, his intellectual dexterity, his muscular stance on being an individual, not just as a gay man, but as a Black man, not just accepting the narrative of what a Black man should be, or could be, just made me completely rethink who I was. What that meant. And it's just stayed with me really to this day. It's really helped me understand my own self-esteem better.

I've watched him debating with white intellectuals on various TV shows in America and I observed that he was seen as something of a freak, because he could debate with them and basically leave them floored at any time. The white people would be quite aggressive with him, and he would just calmly respond, just unravelling their arguments in front of them and the white audience. This is the power of him, really, that he crossed over like many Black artists do. Because he was so good, he crossed over into the mainstream white universe while still retaining his dignity as a Black man. And that's bloody hard to do.

If you want to have influence across and within society at large, you have to speak to the white majority in America. And in this country too because the most dominant creature in the western world is a white middle class man.

There are three stages that Baldwin went through, one of internal recognition, realizing that he did have an interest in reading and writing and intellect. Then racial recognition with Black people telling him he was very clever. They saw him as gifted and beautiful in that sense. And then that gave him the confidence and the platform to demonstrate his eloquence. Baldwin went through all three stages. There are not many Black people who do that, to be honest.

CHERYL: He was ahead of his time in terms of being openly gay and speaking truth to power. Do you think he was frightened?

VICTOR: I'm sure he was terrified.

CHERYL: He had moral courage though, didn't he?

VICTOR: He had total moral courage but also a kind of certainty, to be himself in any circumstance. And that's, you know, self-actualization, I guess, which we all try and achieve. But he had it.

CHERYL: The other thing that I find remarkable is his ability to be forgiving and not to hold hatred.

VICTOR: What he often said in the documentary is that there's no point in just hating the oppressor because that forces you to be like the oppressor. What you need to do is understand the oppressor, and to be yourself in the face of the oppressor. If you can deconstruct the anger and attach it to understanding – that's a hard thing to achieve.

CHERYL: He had a quality of empathy…

VICTOR: Yeah, that kind of empathy is very unusual. You know, there are limits to empathy. I'm actually giving a TED Talk on the limits of empathy. If you understand the reasons why people do things and what drives them, that understanding can only lead to empathy. Very difficult to not have empathy with someone once you understand them. Because ultimately that understanding connects them with your humanity. And then it's very difficult to hate them as well, to be honest.

CHERYL: As a young person were there any role models?

VICTOR: Growing up in Wakefield, Muhammad Ali was huge for me as a role model. I could connect with him as a sportsperson, but it was more his intellect that intrigued me. There weren't many Black people on television, on our screens, who were just bloody clever. You know, not only clever in talking about race but intellectually sparkling. You could listen to him debate with white people and it gave you a sense that it was okay for Black people to think and to be thinkers and writers and engage with society through intellectual discourse as opposed to physical effort.

I started writing poetry when I was five, but at school we were only taught poetry written by dead white people.

CHERYL: So, who did you read? Did you read Derek Walcott or Wole Soyinka?

VICTOR: Yes, Derek Walcott, because I was writing poetry and a little Wole Soyinka because my mother knew him vaguely when she was a kid back in Nigeria. I did, in fact, take the greatest works of Wole Soyinka as my choice on *Desert Island Discs*.

CHERYL: One of the things that's come up is the expectation of mediocrity and how you have to challenge that as a kind of internal barrier. Do you find that is still the case with the young people you meet?

VICTOR: Well, it is still the case. It's the case with my own children and this fact has been researched by, I think, the Sutton Trust. What I witnessed is that the expectations of teachers influence the outcomes of children. I mean, there's no question about it. It's in my own kids. And when I reflect on my education, I now realize I'm not stupid (laughs). I can't be because I wouldn't have been able to do the things that

I've done. But my point is, nobody ever sat me down and said, "Actually, Victor, you're quite smart. Let me put my arm around you and help you navigate your way." Whereas I saw lots of white kids who weren't that smart, who had teachers who helped them to navigate the way.

CHERYL: You've been awarded many honorary degrees now?

VICTOR: Yes, about twenty of them.

CHERYL: Did you ever go to university yourself or not?

VICTOR: No, I didn't. I did eventually go to Northeast London Polytechnic, I did half a degree in Applied Biology, but I dropped out in my third year; I couldn't cope really with it all. I didn't have any money. I had quite a difficult childhood, and I think that affects you in all kinds of strange ways. And I wasn't really gonna be a scientist. So, I dropped out and I remember the head of biology telling me that the last person who dropped out of his course was still sweeping up at Victoria Coach Station, which hardly gave me a lot of confidence in my abilities to make my way in the world. I always felt terrible about dropping out because I ended up in positions where, of course, I was surrounded by people who all had degrees from Oxford and Cambridge. So, I felt like, you know, talk about imposter syndrome... Anyway, at around thirty-six, I thought about whether I should do an MBA or something like that, and eventually I did a master's in Advanced Organizational Consulting at the Tavistock Institute and City University. I haven't got a degree to this day, but I've got a master's (laughs).

CHERYL: How did you get into working at Centrepoint and getting involved in housing and homelessness?

VICTOR: Well, I had a balloon debate with myself about what I *did* want to do. And I decided that Maslow's hierarchies and things associated with them are more important than anything else, so I picked housing (laughs). Because we lived in a house that was condemned for human habitation when I was a kid.

Like many aesthetes I like my surroundings. I'm speaking to you from the House of Lords in the Princess Chamber at the moment.

CHERYL: So, I see. Very grand. Glorious.

VICTOR: Yeah. Very. But when I was a kid, I was a very sensitive kid, and I would cry a lot like at the end of term because I'd imagine that I'd never see my friends again. I used to curse myself because boys weren't supposed to cry. I used to hate it. I used to absolutely hate myself. And then as I got older, I realized it was probably the greatest gift I've ever had because it allowed me to understand what was going on around me. If you are speaking to lots of people, being sensitive to the emotions of other human beings is really powerful.

CHERYL: Did you have an upbringing in the church? Was it important like it was for Baldwin?

VICTOR: It was. I could see that it was important to Baldwin, and it was important to me. Actually, it was more important to my parents. But some people are just born with a question mark, right? My parents were devout Christians, my mother still is, and she uses God and Jesus in every other sentence. It left me with questions like: Why? What is this? (Laughs) So, I read the Bible, the Bhagavad Gita, the Koran, because I was curious. What is this thing that forces these rules and these restrictions and all this stuff? And what is this thing that allows people to behave in bizarre and cruel ways that seem to have nothing to do with what they're saying? It made me feel skeptical of organized religion.

CHERYL: So, it made you recognize hypocrisy?

VICTOR: Well, it's a bit more subtle than that. It was just the inhumanity of rules that prevented you from fully celebrating life. The one thing these religions all have in common is that you must be obedient to someone who doesn't really know if there is a heaven or hell, but he's generally either richer than you or more powerful than you. I guess the notion that we can judge others in that binary way of good and evil doesn't make a lot of sense to me. But it's behind a lot of the rationales for racism and extreme racism.

CHERYL: Coming back to what you said when you watched the documentary *I Am Not Your Negro,* how did it make you re-evaluate your sense of self? Can you just talk a bit more about that? Because you are an incredibly successful person. You are in the House of Lords for example.

VICTOR: Well, okay, so that's a big question. First, people assume that you're successful as a result of the things that you either own or by the titles that you've obtained, right? Or both. People rarely ask you by what method you consider yourself to be successful. So ostensibly, yes, I am successful. I've got a lot of honours but I still don't feel successful because success for me is being totally free to pursue interests that may not relate to the things that I feel passionate about. Is that an odd thing to say? (Laughs)

CHERYL: What do you mean by that?

VICTOR: Well, I feel passionate about a lot of things, such as social justice. But I also feel that if you are a Black man, it's hard to escape the impact of racism, and it's hard to escape the need to fight against it.

But I'd like to be free of that to pursue creative endeavours that aren't necessarily related to, for want of a better term, social good. As I told you, I started writing poetry at five years old. Success for me would be the freedom to explore other parts of myself, including the creative self, which I left behind a bit, but it's a part of me.

I mean, it's not that I would abandon the fight for a just society, it's just that freedom is about being in balance, it's about knowing that you have more choices than the ones given to you by circumstance. And that's what James Baldwin was involved in – that's what he represents, for me.

James Baldwin died a free man.

CHERYL: Well, he had to go and live in the south of France, didn't he?

VICTOR: He did. But that's my point, really. You know, most people who were born where he was born, never freed themselves from that. He used the world to become what he needed to be, and he did achieve a sense of self-actualization. That's what made him so powerful.

CHERYL: In a way he took himself out of his time and out of his place to have perspective on it.

VICTOR: Yeah. To become his true self, to become who he needed to be. We must all escape from where we are to become our true selves. I think it's rare but most great artists achieve it. That's why we think they're great.

The World is White No Longer

Toyin Agbetu

*"People who shut their eyes to reality simply invite
their own destruction, and anyone who insists on
remaining in a state of innocence long after that
innocence is dead turns himself into a monster."*

– James Baldwin, 'Stranger in the Village'[1]

Baldwin was a brilliant writer and political thinker, but to truly
understand the complexity of his genius, it is essential to read
beyond his novels.

Ethnographic Witnessing: On the Lives of Skinfolk

With his mastery of novella as an art form, James "Jimmy"
Baldwin was preoccupied with producing works about African
Americans. Indeed, almost all of his literary output was
involved in depicting, critiquing and analysing the condition
faced by his skinfolk in the USA. His beautiful prose chronicles
the systematic, savage barbarity of the American system
brought to bear on the everyday experience of the African
American. But why? Well, Baldwin answers this when speaking
about the power of orality to communicate ideas that reason
alone cannot reach. In his famous *A Rap on Race* with Margaret
Mead, one of the world's most well-known anthropologists
at the time, he explains that narratives on "History must, in
one way, be a metaphor for the techniques of survival people
have used. And something of that must rest with you forever"
(1971, 106).

---

1 James Baldwin 'Stranger in the Village', *Harper's Magazine*, 1953.

For anthropologists, Baldwin's words invoke frequent comments about how, when writing up their ethnographic encounters after fieldwork, many in the discipline, especially those who engage in reflective practice, are often accused of being honorary or at least amateur novelists. It is common for ethnographers, both in training and practice, to cite Clifford Geertz's article (1973) on 'thick descriptions' to justify offering rich, detailed accounts of the human practices, symbols and behaviours that social anthropologists witness while doing fieldwork. However, when reading the fictional works of Baldwin, I argue it is self-evident that the radical bilingualism demonstrated through his authentic communication of African American vernacular and his profound insights into human identity, social relations, and cultural practices almost qualify him as an honorary anthropologist. His work is thick with description, rich with cultural analysis and simply unforgettable.

Before I studied anthropology, my training as an urban ethnographer came about through a natural curiosity about the nature of power, racism and in particular, Afriphobia (European Parliament 2019). I became an anthropologist when I discovered that the colonial toolkit of the discipline could be reverse-coopted to enable scholar-activist research styles to analyse oppressive political and cultural institutions. Like the protagonists of many of Baldwin's works, I wanted to learn how the grassroots communities I lived amongst and worked with could disrupt the authority of their oppressors. When Baldwin describes his brief stint as a socialist in "The Harlem Ghetto," he simultaneously exhibits a masterful, if not sharp in places, analysis of African Americans' conditions, structures and aspirations throughout the 1940s.

Not all Kinfolk: Dealing with Trauma

Yet, it is when this work is read in tandem with his non-fictional accounts that his writing truly comes alive. Despite

Baldwin's directness on matters of white supremacy, he did his best to maintain a level of objectivity when discussing racism in all its forms. His insightful rendition of Afriphobia, in its external and internalised guises, is best crystalised in his novel *Go Tell It on the Mountain* (1953) and essay collection *Notes of a Native Son* (1955), the missive to his estranged, deceased father. Baldwin exhibits his eloquence while exploring Frantz Fanon's ideas of internalised self-hatred expressed in *Black Skin, White Masks* (1952) and Du Bois' theory of double consciousness *Souls of Black Folk* (1903).

In the lead essay, he explains in a powerful, emotional exposé of a son's relationship with a parent, how his father was "black but did not know he was beautiful." In a single sentence, these poignant words reflect the complexity of Baldwin's relationship with his African heritage, the Baptist church that his preacher father raised him within, and the silent but deadly poison of racism that inhabited the cultural and institutional pores of Harlem. Despite being interested in the plight of African people worldwide. Baldwin deliberately self-defined as a 'black' or, to be specific, a 'Negro' American.

I write this, for whilst possessing a sharp analytical mind, Baldwin also had an acidic tongue. This can be observed in his critical engagement with the principles of Négritude in his report 'Princes and Powers' from the 1956 Congress of Black Writers and Artists in Paris. In it, Baldwin challenges the Pan-Africanist discourse of leading figures like Aimé Césaire and Léopold Sédar Senghor. Baldwin's scornful critique is particularly evident in his portrayal of Césaire's presentation *Culture et Colonisation*, where he describes Césaire as a gifted demagogue with the composure of a jungle cat and a delivery that has a "curious, slow-moving blandness." (Baldwin, 1957).

It was this approach that saw him face derision from many activists who should have made natural bedfellows. This included the likes of Eldridge Cleaver, the Black Panther Party's

Minister of Information. In his book *Soul on Ice*, Cleaver (1968, 124–28) unfairly used Baldwin's honesty about his challenges with self-hatred and homosexual identity to justify writing a harsh critique of the author riddled with toxic masculinity.

This does not mean that Baldwin was without fault. In his own words, Baldwin was not what he called a 'race' man. In fact, as a social critic, he was scathing of not only established 'negro leaders' but also, perhaps, unfairly critical of entertainers who engaged in political activity such as Paul Robeson whom he dubbed as bitter and 'un-American'. As a consequence, Baldwin's disdain for the Pan-African movement saw some of his kinfolk accusing him of being an integral part of the bourgeoisie that he critiqued as "middle-class darkies". Sadly, it would leave him isolated by activists and artists alike.

However, it is crucial to recognise that Baldwin's dissent against Pan-Africanism and the notion of the existence of a unified, pre-Maafa African culture, as suggested by scholars like Cheikh Anta Diop, stems from his belief that the colonial experience was instrumental in cultivating literate, civilised continental Africans. In contrast, he argued that the identity and culture of African Americans were influenced by and, despite the violence which he detested, somewhat birthed by their experience of enslavement in the Americas. In the opening autobiographical section of *Notes of a Native Son*, Baldwin wrote that his loathing of 'black people' arose because they "failed to produce Rembrandt". There is no indication that he was being ironic.

Radical Creative: Writing Wrongs while Dreaming of Love

However, none of this detracts from the brilliance of his writing, which was inspired by his early exposure to the writing of Ralph Ellison. As an artist, Baldwin sought to transcend the limits of the 'protest novel' and in bringing the oppressed and oppressor together, attempted to normalise ideas of African American humanity. Baldwin revealed that he not only understood human values, structures, and beliefs but was also able to offer critiques of cultural practices through his works. Indeed, through his books like *The Fire Next Time*, Baldwin demonstrated an understanding of anthropology's core principles and concepts whenever he critically examined the cultural norms perpetuating racial inequality, and in particular, Afriphobia in America.

The same was true in his public discussions and interviews, as it was with his writing. For example, if we continue to examine his discussion with Mead, their talk on 'race' and society revealed the synergy between them and the intellectual fractures that continue to exist between colonial and decolonial forms of anthropology (1971). Whereas Mead considered "the domination of the white world over the rest of the world [as] a short accident of history," Baldwin focused on how societal institutions shape individual identities and experiences, and by simultaneously providing a historical context to these matters, he even highlighted how past events shape present realities. His novel, *If Beale Street Could Talk* (1974) explores this theme extensively.

So, what makes Baldwin a role model for decolonial scholars such as myself? Is it his ability to engage in cultural relativism? Baldwin certainly excelled at exploring, living, and sharing details on countercultural practices without framing them as backward or somehow deviant. I loved that he understood and empathised with the theories and lived experiences of people from different backgrounds which said otherwise. From a methodological perspective, he engaged in the practice of immersing himself in the world of a city-based research community to gain first-hand knowledge and understanding of their culture. I would later learn that writers like W.E.B. Du Bois pioneered the field of urban ethnography that would later school famous anthropologists like Franz Boas, who in turn, taught both the novelist Zora Neale Hurston, and indeed, Margaret Mead.

However, I think it is his exceptional ability to use critical thinking skills to question prevailing beliefs about human behaviour that makes his ideas relevant to all social scientists interested in why certain groups are marginalised or oppressed based on their race, sexuality, or social status. Baldwin was unafraid to observe, analyse, and critique societal norms from within. His essay, 'Stranger in the Village', is a prime example of his ethnographic approach, not only on matters of 'race' but also on topics like sexuality, which he explored in his novel *Giovanni's Room* (1956).

We don't need to guess at how Baldwin saw himself. He explicitly tells us he was a revolutionary at fifteen but gave that up when he stopped being a preacher after leaving the church and adopted a conservative perspective on life. But throughout his journey, he never gave up on challenging racism or structural violence and championing the cause of African Americans. Baldwin claimed the mantle of poet, the subversive scourge of Plato's Republic and a disturber of the peace. Moreover, in his discussion with Mead, Baldwin claims Frederick Douglass along with his righteous indignation and moral clarity as his ancestor. I like that.

You see in my attempt to offer a portrait of the 'other' Baldwin, not the novelist or public intellectual, but the complex, polemical iconoclast, I hope my reflections have helped explain why, despite being widely respected, he deserved to be more accepted by his community. As a Pan-Africanist who admires his legacy, I respect and pay tribute to a legend who far too often downplayed his significant contribution to the development of civil rights for African Americans.

Nevertheless, I still don't know if Baldwin would have liked me had we met. To Baldwin, I would have been a radical 'race' man similar to the African French folk he met in Paris who were confident in their African heritage and identity. To me, he would be a charming representative of the privileged

African American bourgeoisie, struggling, in his own words, to recognise and secure a 'birthright' to make attractive (2017:125). Yet, does it matter?

Baldwin would eventually disavow himself of the notion of proximity to whiteness having a civilising effect. However, this came at the tragic cost of being forced to witness America's terrifying persecution of the Black Panther movement, endure the pain of losing his friend, the NAACP civil rights activist Medgar Evers to murder by white supremacists, and later both Martin Luther King Jr and Malcolm X (later el-Hajj Malik el-Shabazz) to similar assassinations (Winks 2013, 611–12). It changed him.

With Baldwin's penchant for urban ethnography and mine for anthropology, we shared similar concerns, passion and fury over the international plight of African people on issues of racialised injustice and structural violence. Hence, despite our ideological differences, I believe we would probably have developed a strong bond of solidarity, especially when united against a common foe. Kind of like when his 'black' Americans met 'brown' Africans and dared to paint the world in every colour, synthesising what Baldwin referred to as the possibilities of theory and the impossibilities of life in a world that is "white no longer" and never will be again.

> "one must also recognize that morality is based
> on ideas and that all ideas are dangerous –
> dangerous because ideas can only lead to action
> and where the action leads no man can say."
>
> – James Baldwin, 'Stranger in the Village'

Bibliography

1. James Baldwin, 'Stranger in the Village', *Harper's Magazine*, 1953, https://harpers.org/archive/1953/10/stranger-in-the-village/)

2. James Baldwin, *Notes of a Native Son,* Boston: Beacon Press, 1955.

3. James Baldwin, *No Name in the Street*, New York: Dial Press, 1972.

4. James Baldwin, 'Princes and Powers', *Encounter*, January, 1957. https://www.amherst.edu/system/files/media/0239/James_Baldwin__Princes_and_Powers.pdf

5. Eldridge Cleaver, *Soul on Ice*. 1st ed. New York: Dell, 1968. https://archive.org/details/soulonicebyeldridgecleaver

6. W.E.B. Du Bois, *The Souls of Black Folk,* Chicago: A.C. McClurg and Co., 1953. https://www.gutenberg.org/files/408/408-h/408-h.htm

7. European Parliament, 'European Parliament Resolution of 26 March 2019 on Fundamental Rights of People of African Descent in Europe', 26 March 2019. https://www.europarl.europa.eu/doceo/document/TA-8-2019-0239_EN.html

8. Frantz Fanon, *Peau noire masques blancs,* Points Essais 26, Paris: Éd. du Seuil, 1952.

9. Clifford Geertz, *The Interpretation of Cultures: Selected Essays,* Basic Books, 1973.

10. Margaret Mead and James Baldwin, *A Rap on Race*, Philadelphia, Lippincott, 1971.

11. Christopher Winks, 'Into the Heart of the Great Wilderness: Understanding Baldwin's Quarrel with Négritude', *African American Review* 2013, 46 (4): 605–14. https://doi.org/10.1353/afa.2013.0096

James Baldwin presenting a new book at the American Hotel in
Amsterdam, 1974. Photo: Rob Croes/Anefo

"You think your pain and your heartbreak are
unprecedented in the history of the world,
but then you read."

– James Baldwin

Uncle Jimmy's Calling

Rosanna Amaka

There was much inequality – unexplained
Invisible chains that wrangled people in
'It's all in your mind my dear – there are no chains'
And I searched
Kept asking
But why?
'It's of your people's making my dear'
But why?
'Must you concentrate on such things?'
But why?
'It's just the way your people are?'
And the chains?
'There are no chains my dear.'
Then why are so many dying?
'Look what you've done, you're making me cry my dear'
I'm sorry.
'What about my pain my dear?'
But they're dying
'Forget about that my dear,
I much prefer it when you're jolly and you ape around
Make me happy
Dance for me my dear!'

Uncle Jimmy's Calling

'Yes, much better now
You're much more likeable when you ape around'
It's late
Better go
'Must you my dear?'
Uncle Jimmy's calling
'What for my dear?'
Left me something
'Really, my dear?'
It's waiting
And so I left
Ran
As fast as I could
Touched my prized possessions that called me home
From the 'Notes of a Native Son'
To 'The Fire Next Door'
And a few more beside
All spread out neatly on my bed
And in those books I found answers
In those books he articulated what I knew to be true
That, at the time, I did not know how to express aloud
An opening into the arcane ways of the world

The Spirit of James Baldwin

Michelle Yaa Asantewa

When James Baldwin reframes the Socratic dictum about "the unexamined life" and its bearing on his purpose as a writer he simultaneously locates an ancient African philosophy observed by spiritual practitioners of the Yoruba Ifa spiritual system. The concept of Iwa Pele – good character – connects the individual with the far-reaching purpose for which they took up the mantle of an individuated material expression of the Supreme Creative Being, whom the Yoruba call Oludumare. By living to a higher purpose and reflecting Iwa Pele, the individual journeys towards spiritual alignment with that cosmic force. In this way, the individual is esteemed by the honour of a deity through their good conduct and exemplary contributions to humanity.

There are many deities, 'Orisa' in the Ifa system, which are also identified as forces of nature such as water, wind, fire, lightning, and thunder. Each deity has their devotees identified as that energy with which they have specific personal relationships. Baba Esu is a principal Orisa to whom beneficence must be bestowed before consulting all others. His function is as a 'messenger,' whose symbol of the crossroads signifies choices, decisions and challenges. For this reason, he is often misinterpreted as wicked, evil and mischievous. Examined more deeply, one observes that his integrity as the bearer of messages on behalf of humans to Oludumare means he insists on there being a thorough self-examination worthy of the significance of his intermediary function.

The Spirit of James Baldwin

James Baldwin, the self-affirmed witness of the personal and collective pain, deprivation and injustices endured by Africans in a racist America, has similarities with the energy of Baba Esu. James Baldwin opens the way for self-awareness and critical self-evaluation by vociferously challenging us to examine our lives, our humanity, and our struggles to survive. This reading of Baldwin articulates how he functions as an Esu energy that inspires us to relearn the art, beauty and transformative power of love. James Baldwin's literary and prophetic brilliance is, for me, not so much seen or heard, but felt as a potent energy. Descriptions, depictions and concepts about Baba Esu are so abundant as to be overwhelming in a simple search on the internet. It is accepted that he is a messenger who bears messages between Oludumare and human beings, standing therefore as a bridge between us and the divine creative force. It is accepted too that before making offerings to other Orisa we do so to Baba Esu first since he is that bridge.

Varied perceptions about him proliferate because there is a slipperiness inherent in his essential qualities. He is both jovial yet full of wrath, which has been misconceived as 'evil' by white, Western observers. They have associated his complex force with Loki in Norse mythology, with tricksterism, and ultimately he has been likened to the Christian concept of a 'devil.' The dynamic and humanistic Ifa system holds no such binary ideas about good versus evil or God versus the Devil. There are simply routes, paths, progressive and digressive journeyings toward the advanced self – we might readily understand this as the fulfilment of our destiny – more accurately – our 'ori'. When individuals begin to arise in consciousness, they intuitively seek a better exploration of their destiny. They use all forces and phenomena available, inherent in the universe, seen and unseen, toward that end.

Thus, the energy of Baba Esu opens the way, preparing us for spiritual awakenings and the expansion of consciousness.

He is bearing our messages to Oludumare but he may also reveal unwelcome truths if an individual strays from the path of behaving in good character, with full humanity.

Baldwin saw himself as a 'witness,' which we can easily link to Baba Esu's messenger profile. His role as witness means that he could not isolate himself into any one narrative or construction of being human. The obsession with single narratives, which is altogether limiting with the incumbent desire to categorise, squanders a quality which is vital in understanding a presence like Baldwin in our world. I call this quality our spiritual intelligence. It operates when one can look at someone and see beyond their physical appearance. When we are able to acknowledge the spirit of an individual, we are sharpening our spiritual intelligence. This enables us to align with the life-giving force through which we are ourselves creative, thereby advancing in consciousness, aiming toward our higher selves, our divinity. It should not therefore surprise us when Baldwin's biographer, David Leeming, writes that: "It was the calling to bear witness to the truth that dominated Baldwin's being, and in this role he could be harsh, uncompromising, and even brutally cruel" (1994:xii). The truth is sometimes uncompromising and brutal depending on the receptivity of the heart or conscience to which it is directed. Much of Baldwin's 'harsh, uncompromising' truth is directed at white Americans. In his essay 'Everybody's Protest Novel' he slates writer Harriet Beecher Stowe's iconic book *Uncle Tom's Cabin*:

"The spirit that breathes in this book, hot, self-righteous fearful, is not different from that spirit of medieval times which sought to exorcise evil by burning witches; and is not different from that terror which activates a lynch mob." (1955:18). This is a scathing critique of a book considered a classic anti-slavery, protest novel of the 19th century. Baldwin otherwise challenges its premise and the writer's motives in a way that might be regarded as 'harsh' and brutal. Although in the same essay he is also critical of Richard Wright's *Native Son* (1955:22), Baldwin's main target was the mythology of the American nation – and the self-delusion of white Americans – whose continuing discrimination against African Americans created a sense of privilege which they wanted to uphold. His exposure of their guilty conscience in relation to the enslavement by their forefathers of African people would naturally be considered brutally cruel.

The central question posed to the American people, which Raoul Peck so masterfully determines at the end of the documentary *I Am Not Your Negro*, is to ask why white Americans needed to invent the 'N-word?' This question ought to be forever etched on the psyche of white people who sought to conquer the souls of Africans to justify their economic exploitation of African bodies and labour. The question is not asked because Africans in America and other parts of the diaspora, want to wallow in victimhood or trauma, rather than discover strategies to oppose the most recent forms of oppression and domination that Black people continue to face.

Instead of dealing with this question of their construction of Black people as less than human there is an obsession with Baldwin the man – and particularly his sexuality. At the screening of *I Am Not Your Negro* at Phoenix Cinema in 2017, where I joined Tony Warner to conduct the Q&A, this was the first question from a white professor in the audience: "Why was there an absence of his sexuality in the film?" Some years ago, the first time I was invited to do a Q&A on Baldwin at the British Film Institute's screening of Dick Fontaine's *I Heard It Through the Grapevine* (1982), the first question was again centred around Baldwin's sexuality, which was not the focus of either documentary. Often the fixation on his sexuality makes no mention of an adolescent 'violation' – at about age fourteen – when he was fondled by an older man, which both aroused and terrified the young Baldwin. But Baldwin's 'witnessing' is total; he was aware, of course, that adolescence presupposes evocative and evolutionary experiences that individuals choose to take with them through their life journeys or leave behind. Sometimes those experiences haunt us like shadows dancing at every turn of our lives, sometimes they liberate us from limited perspectives about what it means to be human. I would agree with Leeming that Baldwin was at times 'ambivalent' about his sexuality (1994:xiii). This can be linked to his self-styling role as 'witness' but this ambivalence could also be linked to his shape-shifting spirit as Baba Esu. Cursory readings about Baba Esu reveal things like his love of sex, alcohol, fun, cigarettes, dancing, etc. (Neimark 1993:72). He is not attempting to please, appease, nor deliberately disparage by being this or that thing. He is a balancer of forces, if you will, redeeming polar extremes when necessary to set us back on track. Baldwin's ambivalent sexuality is expressed through the bisexuality of his characters which demonstrates his understanding of human needs and desires. He does not judge his characters for their transgressions, but rather permits us to understand them through his empathetic descriptions of their inner worlds.

It's certain, as Douglas Field considers, that Baldwin's "reputation has suffered from his refusal to adhere to a single ideology and his continued resistance to, and suspicion of, labels and categories" (2009:4). His critics, both Black and white, wanted him to choose a position – identify himself as homosexual or heterosexual, be an essayist or novelist, live in USA or Europe, be a spokesperson for civil rights or a celebrity of white America's illusions about 'the Negro,' be a Negro/Black writer or a literary writer. But no 'prophet,' as Leeming has called him, would claim to be this or that given that the pendulum of human transgressions is ever in flux. Spirit is thrifty, adapting to myriad movements at the same time. According to Leeming, Baldwin was a prophet not so much in the tradition of foreseeing events – although *The Fire Next Time* (1963) bears witness to the fact that he sometimes did precisely that – he understood like prophets in the Bible that as a witness he must stand alone in anger against a nation that seemed intent on not 'keeping the faith' (1994:xiii). The nature of this faith is simple: every human being deserves the right to exist without fear of deliberate and systematic attempts to deny them every possible chance of survival.

"I am not a nigger," he boldly declares on the screen, "I am a man." And that persistent struggle to be acknowledged as equal and not 'other' or 'less than', as Field observes, occupied his literary explorations throughout his lifetime, and is especially signalled in book titles like *Nobody knows My Name*, *No Name in the Street* and the essay title 'Stranger in the Village' (Field, 2009:9).

Peck's documentary emphasises a causal relationship between persistent racism and white supremacy, through its collaging of footage from the 1960s Civil Rights movement and the Black Lives Matter movement, sixty years later. But Baldwin's spirit does not speak passionately only to white supremacists but to those liberals who are so complacent in their privilege that they are unable to see how their silence on matters of unprecedented white on Black racist killings makes them complicit in the degenerate actions of their forefathers and contemporary brothers.

During the *I Am Not Your Negro* screening at Phoenix Cinema, a friend said that she endured running commentary by two white women behind her making comments like "it's so biased, not all white people are like that." During the Q&A, in response to a question, I said that Africans were disproportionately incarcerated, and a large number have mental ill-health issues. One of the white women seated behind my friend muttered: "I think you'll find they're asylum seekers." I wondered why they were there if they weren't prepared to allow the brainstem to properly perform its function of relaying information that would enable them to gain a deeper understanding of how discrimination works.

Encounters with James Baldwin

Baldwin's critics wanted some barometer by which to measure him. For a time, they compared him with other 'negro writers' like Ralph Ellison and Richard Wright. But Baldwin's refusal to be pigeonholed caused critics to overlook his literary worth which might explain the lack of literary recognition for his work during his lifetime.

The father symbol appears in a lot of Baldwin's work. His first book *Go Tell It on the Mountain* (1953), about a boy preacher who challenges his authoritarian preacher father is autobiographical. He did not know his biological father; he knew only Reverend David Baldwin, the man his mother, Emma Berdis Jones, married when he was about three and with whom he had many battles. He contemplated these battles with his stepfather throughout his lifetime, as powerfully rendered in the essay, 'Notes of a Native Son.' He had imagined he hated his stepfather but later recognised that his stepfather's weaknesses, parading as authority and power, lay in the pervading psychology of racism that made it impossible for him to love himself and therefore to fully transmit that love to his children. His stepfather's psychic debilitation – he died of tuberculosis in a mental institution – was rooted in the brutal experiences of trying to survive in a world that white people violently declared was theirs.

David Baldwin was frigid around white people, for he felt that they had power over him. Baldwin resented how he acted around their authority. His stepfather had hooked himself onto their model of civilising order – Christianity – but could not transcend his circumstances on earth through its doctrines. For this doctrine taught him that salvation could come only through death, in the milk and honey land of heaven concocted for Black people to accept their earthly servitude while white people enjoyed the double experience of gorging on the nectar both on earth and in heaven.

Esu is also a father symbol, a Baba. Baldwin did not have

children of his own but carried the essence and desire of a father as part of the witness/messenger persona. This was not least because he was the eldest of nine children whom he assisted his mother in raising, but in his role as witness he considered himself somewhat fatherly because of his single-minded mission to "save others through the word" (Leeming, 1994:4). In the present mindboggling and dispirited moment when 'keeping the faith' of advancing humanity is up close and contentious in our lives, the spirit of Baldwin is a timeless indicator that we need healing – a prerequisite for keeping the faith. We might add another question to that which Peck's documentary poses: Why do American and European imperialists need to fuel wars? We might also ask how is it justifiable for a country to arbitrarily bomb other nations without any provocation?

Baldwin was a pacifist whose conscience would err towards human progressiveness, not backwardness, degeneracy and destruction. His words berate and chastise us into seeing sense, that our collective destiny is to advance our humanity, not compete with one other, especially with ever-increasing methods of destruction. James Baldwin reminds us of our human failures – how well can anyone 'keep the faith' when war, and conflicts of a physical, spiritual, mental nature, are always deliberately conceived to disturb the peace? Baldwin can be likened to the ever-chastising Baba Esu, due to his ability to speak truth to power and his belief that a return to the 'faith' lay in humanity's ability to embrace the power of love and forgiveness, forever swinging on the pendulum of human transgressions.

The intuitive feeling I have for Baldwin as Baba Esu penetrated that much deeper when I learnt that a Yoruba death drum opened the celebration at his funeral, attended by 5,000 people who might not have known his name but at last could feel the rhythm and power of his eloquent words.

Bibliography
1. James Baldwin, *Notes of a Native Son*, Boston: Beacon Press, 1955.
2. Douglas Field, ed. *A Historical Guide to James Baldwin*, New York: Oxford University Press, 2009.
3. David Leeming, *James Baldwin – A biography,* London: Michael Joseph, 1994.
4. Philip John Neimark, *The Way of the Orisa: Empowering Your Life Through the Ancient African Religion of Ifa, New York:* Harper San Francisco, 1993.
5. Randall Kenan, 'James Baldwin, 1924–1987 – a brief biography' in *A Historical Guide to James Baldwin* edited by Douglas Field, New York: Oxford University Press, 2009.

Mea Culpa

Eugen Bacon

Once upon a time guilt was a day when reason got nothing done and the silver sun refused to gleam. Dusk fell with the fervour of a night runner who launched at you with juju smelted in your dreams and transgressions without which you could have saved one person – yourself or Mother Africa. Your follies were precisely:

no comment

an ineptitude for parables

inexistence on the fence

and maddening the hell

out of poor people.

James Baldwin (left) with his friend, the painter, Beauford Delaney
(right) in a Paris bar c. 1965. Photographer unknown

Meeting Jimmy Baldwin in Paris

Lindsay Barrett

In 1963, the Café Le Tournon was just across from the gate of the French Senate on the edge of the Quartier Latin on the left bank of the Seine when I first joined the community of exiled poets, painters, jazz musicians, and authors from the Americas in the French capital. It was the nightly venue for an informal gathering of exiled artists and I heard that it had been one of the regular haunts of the African American novelist Richard Wright who had died three years earlier.

Richard Wright's iconic novel *Native Son* had played a large part in encouraging me to pursue a career as a teller of tales based on my observations of Jamaican life and history. I had read the *Ebony* magazine report of his life and death in Paris with deep wonder while I was still in Jamaica in 1960. Two years later, at just over twenty years of age, I visited Paris for the first time while completing my first novel titled, *And When They Killed Him.*

By the time I returned to the fabled city of light in 1963 I had made up my mind that I would rather live there than in London. I'd been struck as if by lightning when, at the age of fifteen, I'd read the novel *Brother Man* written by Jamaica's legendary storyteller Roger Mais, who had lived in Paris as both painter and novelist in the mid-1950s. Mais had paid a memorable visit to All Saints Elementary school in Matthews Lane in downtown Kingston, Jamaica, when I was a ten-year -old Class Three pupil there. When I told one of my uncles that I intended to be a writer like Mais, he told me this was a very positive aim and that set the trajectory of my life's course at the time. As a consequence, whenever I read novels at that impressionable age, I took an interest in finding out anything I could about the author's biographical background.

On my second visit to Paris, James Baldwin's name was everywhere, especially after the publication of a brilliant collection of essays titled *Notes of a Native Son,* which had interrogated the cultural and philosophical presumptions of Richard Wright's bestselling narratives. I had enjoyed reading the essays because they read like poetry with a depth of emotional intensity that I particularly admired. I had also read his major novel *Go Tell It on the Mountain,* and been impressed by the descriptive accuracy of its setting and the rhetorical accuracy of its conversational content.

A few months before my return to Paris the famous bilingual literary journal *Two Cities* had published an impressionistic reflection of mine about a trip I had taken to post-war Germany. I had tried to adopt the Baldwin method of commentary and reflection in that work. The journal had paid me nothing but I was given a few copies of the publication which I could attempt to sell for about ten francs each. That was what took me to the Café Le Tournon one night when I saw a crowd of very agitated people gathered at a sidewalk table. I handed out a few copies of the journal to some of them without really noticing who they were and then someone asked me to sit with them. It was only then that I noticed a diminutive but excited individual to whom the whole table seemed to be listening. He asked me if I was the author of the piece about journeying through Germany and I said I was. He then said he had read it a few days before and that he was very impressed. I did not know as yet who he was and so his comment, while pleasing, did not have much effect.

I was accompanied that night by a new friend I had made,

a former US G.I. and poet named John Poncet, and it was he who whispered to me that it was James Baldwin.

When he told me, I immediately felt a shock of both surprise and exultation, and I began to thank Baldwin for his kind words. He laughed when I tried to express what must have seemed like very naïve gratitude and asked me if I had more work to show him. I then said that I was working on my first novel and he asked me if he could have a look at it. I told him that I was not sure that it was ready and he said to me that my hesitancy was a good sign since every writer should be critical of their own work. Nevertheless, he gave me his hotel address on the Right Bank and suggested that I should have lunch with him the following day.

I didn't make it to the lunch date and a few weeks later I burnt the manuscript of my novel and started another one which was to eventually become *Song for Mumu,* my first novel to be published. However, that was the first of quite a few meetings I had with James Baldwin over the next three years during my time in Paris. In one of these meetings I told him of the influence that my grandmother had on me by telling me Bible stories and Anansi tales. He told me that he had been influenced strongly by Bible stories as well and that those of us who had grown up in religious homes were prone to become writers.

Jean Fanchette, the editor and publisher of *Two Cities,* was surprised when a fortnight or so after the Café Le Tournon meeting he received a message from Hoyt Fuller, the Chicago-based editor of the *Negro Digest* asking to be put in touch with me. When I spoke with Fuller by telephone he told me that James Baldwin had suggested that I might be a good contributor to the *Digest.* A few months later, Fuller paid a visit to Paris and this led to the publication of several of my essays and short stories and eventually led to me winning the Conrad Kent Rivers Memorial Prize.

James Baldwin's book-length essay *The Fire Next Time*

appeared in *The New Yorker* magazine later that year and it had an incredible impact on the work of those of us living in Paris and trying to remain relevant to public opinion in our homelands.

I left Paris early in 1966 to attend the Festival of Black and African Arts and Culture in Senegal, and when that event ended, I decided that I would visit other countries in West Africa starting with Sierra Leone. Although I did not keep in touch with Baldwin, his introduction to the editor of the *Negro Digest,* which had by then been renamed the *Black Digest,* had made my name familiar to some members of the West African academic community. It was this that helped me make up my mind to be domiciled, at least for a time, in Nigeria, and although I never heard from James Baldwin again, my long sojourn in West Africa might owe a debt of gratitude to him for that profound encounter at the Café Tournon where a celebrated author expressed genuine appreciation for the work of a naïve and hesitant young apprentice.

The Café Le Tournon in Saint-Germain des Prés, Paris.
Photo: D. Berretty. See: www. letournon.com

Genius as Moral Courage

Gabriella Beckles-Raymond

I don't quite remember when I first read James Baldwin. Sometimes genius enters one's life in a blaze of wonder. At other times it just creeps in, lingers for a while and becomes part of the fabric of your being without you realising quite when or how. This is how James Baldwin came to me. I might have discovered Baldwin as a teen when I fell in love with my local Black bookshop, one on Quex Road in Kilburn, North West London, and another at the home of legendary activist bookseller, Pepukayi, or it could have been when I was at Morgan State University, basking in the wonder of being at a historically Black university, where the content of English literature classes finally included the works of people like me. And yet I feel that wherever or whenever it was, there was a kind of ordained inevitability that our paths would cross because anyone interested in truth or who has, as Baldwin put it, "a devotion to the human being, his freedom and fulfilment,"[1] must sit with him at some point. For me, Baldwin is essential to that project of fulfilment of what it means to Liv Good,[2] precisely because he understands the difference between devotion to the human being and devotion to humanity, "which is too easily equated with a devotion to a Cause; and Causes, as we know, are notoriously bloodthirsty."[3]

---

1 James Baldwin, *Collected Essays*, edited by Toni Morrison, New York: Library of America, 1988, p.12.
2 For a description of 'Liv Good' see Gabriella Beckles-Raymond, '"Liv Good": Dreaming the Intersectionally-Just Good Life.' *Feminist Review*, 2024, 137:1-18.
3 Baldwin, *op. cit*, p.12.

Such acute distinctions, characteristic of his writing, are part of why Baldwin's work is recognisable as genius. Indeed, how can one ignore timelessly poignant analyses offered in *Notes of a Native Son*; the rich vulnerability of *Giovanni's Room*, the unflinching truths of *The Fire Next Time*, and the powerful dexterity of not only his overall body of written work but also of his interviews and debates? However, in the context of how our society sees genius, James Baldwin invites us to understand the term differently – to assert genius as moral courage. Genius understood in terms of moral courage and exemplified by Baldwin, entails a holistic set of cognitive, emotional, spiritual skills, which grant us the ability to see past the myth of society's lies and hold oneself and others to account in honouring truth and love. Such vision requires an alternative way of knowing.

On Genius

I often hear people with remarkable intellectual abilities described as genius. Fair enough. But such an ethically unqualified definition leaves the door open for what has become normalised as a prevailing trope in literature and media in our society – the idea of the evil genius – that person whose mind is allegedly so brilliant, that we show no surprise at the dangerous moral implications of their intellectual contributions. Machiavelli and Hitler are often noted as archetypal examples. We glorify the amoral when it's accompanied by dominant power, reward it with attention, money, position and more power. Overcoming this lack of regard for the moral in our understanding of genius is necessary if we are to have a more meaningful conception of genius.

Ultimately, what is being rewarded is what I call 'Rational Manliness' – subscription to Western norms of race, class, gender, sexuality, religion, ability and age.[4] No one knew

4 Gabriella Beckles-Raymond, 'Rational Manliness as Goodness: Responses to Intersectional Domination and the Preservation of the Moral Self in Higher Education' *Journal of ABPN,* 2021, 13 (37).

this better than James Baldwin – Black, gay, poor – who was intimately confronted by intersectional injustice, in addition to having to live through the assassinations of three of the great moral leaders of his time in Medgar Evers, Martin Luther King and Malcolm X, all of whom he knew personally. Those who seek to love the human being, those who are truth tellers, those who seek to enlarge us aesthetically and spiritually, our society does not reward but rather seeks to kill, destroy, discredit, humiliate, either with state violence or by a death of a thousand cuts. Baldwin knew this and brought his pen to bear witness anyway.

In a world where Rational Manliness prevails, Blackness is antithetical to genius. People racialised as Black can be noble savages but not noble geniuses. Similarly, we can be stupid and evil as these are key to Euro-modernity's definition of Blackness, but we cannot be evil geniuses because genius is only recognised insofar as it tends towards whiteness. Sometimes Black genius is recognised but typically only in fields that we are stereotypically known to be good at like music and sports. Even then, genius is ascribed in accordance with the ability to capture the 'cross-over' market rather than on its own cultural terms, as if these can be separated from genius.

For the non-musical, non-white, non-male prospective genius, we too must cross over. We can only access the qualifier 'genius' when we attend 'prestigious' universities as demonstration of our intellectual prowess; hone our professional skills in multinational companies that are destroying the global south, and have our brilliance confirmed only when we have thoroughly demonstrated our complicity with the aims of Rational Manliness.

Similarly, it is not a coincidence that women, while often represented as evil, are not typically presented as genius both because of their gender and lack of systemic power. Think of the biblical conception of Eve within colonial Christianity, the staples of English children's literature and the Disney cartoon canon which promote this trope at the earliest stages of childhood consciousness. Women can be wicked witches and evil stepmothers and even the root cause of all sin in the world but such caricatures, despite their capacity to control the intellect of men, the mysteries of nature and the power of the gods, are not credited with the status of being genius. Furthermore, archetypes of evilness work differently depending on whether a woman is racialised as white or Black. The category evil is designed to track an aberration within the group – human beings. Insofar as people racialised as Black are dehumanised and assumed morally degenerate, there is no anomaly to identify.

On Moral Courage

As Baldwin rightly observed, "It has always been much easier (because it has always seemed much safer) to give a name to the evil without than to locate the terror within."[5] Baldwin's brilliance was in his willingness and ability to grapple with the terror within, not as a form of narcissism but as the necessary force that enables social transformation. As such, his example offers us a different model of genius altogether. James Baldwin reminds us that moral courage must be central to any meaningful definition of genius.

Courage is typically understood as a virtue, a character trait that enables us to be strong in the face of fear or danger. It often functions as a substitute for bravery of a very patriarchal kind, which individualistically valorises the likes of soldiers who face the horrors of war. Such individualism confines courage to a direct correspondence with emotion, whether it is about overcoming fear or rendering it altogether invisible. More fitting as a description of Baldwin, of those he witnessed being murdered and of those whose lives were destroyed and whom history chooses not to remember, is a courage whose point of reference was more structural. It is of less relevance

5 Baldwin, op. cit, p. 694.

to the meaning of courage whether Medgar and Martin and Malcolm felt afraid or chose to overcome or dismiss their fear or the danger they themselves faced. What matters more was the state of terror in which such individuals and, crucially, those they loved, were made to live. However, in the Western context, both courage and moral courage have come to be entangled. Can one overcome one's fears and be strong in the face of danger, whether that be physical or moral?

If the dangers we face are features of Westernised society – racism, patriarchy, poverty, bigotry – we need a qualitatively different kind of courage. Cognitively, moral courage entails the ability and insistence to accurately describe the condition in which humans find themselves relative to their true purpose and its relationship to the ways in which society is structured. Such moral perception rests on a worldview that requires the kind of education one does not get in school, limited as it is by what Baldwin described as the paradox of education, "designed to perpetuate the aims of society", even as "one begins to examine the society in which he is being educated."[6] Moral courage demands that we learn from the multiple different sources of information available to a human being as Baldwin did – the streets, the church, our emotions (one's own and others'), the spirit as well as more conventional avenues like books and listening to elders. In so doing, we activate multiple ways of coming to know the contradictions of society that stand between our capacity to live freely and our oppressed condition, not merely as deviant features of an otherwise neutral or enshrined society but at a level that indicts society as fundamentally broken. In the context of a global order that works tirelessly to distort our reality, cultivating the ability to see what is real and true, to dare to name our everyday terrors, is a skill worth treasuring.

Emotionally, activating this skill requires the strength to

---

6 Baldwin, *ibid*, p.678.

take personal responsibility for the societies we have created. Throughout his work, Baldwin had the fortitude to open himself up to profound vulnerability, to risk the destruction of his very self, not in a pathological, self-destructive way, but in a reflexive mode of being that understood and was committed to examine that terror within, to choose life over death (social, moral, spiritual, and physical) to grapple with what it means to be a human being. Importantly, however, Baldwin showed that the emotional aspect also resists the individualistic reading so easily rendered onto all things human in today's society. His consistent will to confront and stand by and for the truth regardless of the personal cost was based on seeing this very truth as the price and source of human freedom. Genius of this kind demands radical openness to others – to keep being determined to connect and reach out, to forgive and to re-connect, and to give grace and understanding, even when one is misunderstood, rejected, unwelcome and devalued. Moreover, as Baldwin reminds us, unlike dominatory power, the power of vulnerability is available to us all – his genius was not unique in its essence, rather it was exemplary.

In this vein, moral courage necessarily entails a spiritual dimension, which commits its genius to being in relation to a higher power and which drives the conviction to live in service of humans. Even as Baldwin eschewed religion, he was clearly rooted in the spirituality of his church upbringing. This he often expressed in terms of love – not sentimental, romantic love as we have grown accustomed to imagining, but radical and revolutionary love. As Baldwin explains, "I conceive of God, in fact, as a means of liberation and not a means to control others."[7] As such, Baldwin's work and life teach us that moral genius is about that ethical activism, answering the call of love. Baldwin further explains, "Love is a battle, love is a war, love is a growing up."[8] If we take Baldwin's point about growth seriously, moral genius entails consistency over time,

7 Ibid. p.220.
8 Ibid. p.220.

which is evidenced when we are in it for the long haul, no matter the setbacks, resisting sentimentality, escapism and the enticements of Western versions of success.

Indeed, Baldwin insisted we recognise our interdependence and shared existence. What defines genius, then, is not that danger or fear or material rewards and accolades drive us to respond, but rather that we are moved by our spiritual conviction to human beings (including ourselves), to the environment, and to a higher power.

Genius as Moral Courage

Therefore, regardless of one's purported intellectual prowess, exceptional skills, or systemic power, to use those talents for ill, to feign a sense of responsibility even as we refuse the truth, to refuse to grow even as we celebrate progress, to choose death over love, should not in any version of the term, be defined as genius. James Baldwin's legacy and indeed his genius is that he lived his life as the most godlike manifestation of his being and through his work and example invited us to do the same. Not only did he survive the brutality of what it means to be poor, Black, gay and a writer in America, he spent his lifetime penning and speaking truth to power courageously, beautifully, unapologetically so that we may learn to love. He is for me, the true definition of genius.

"The place in which I'll fit will not exist until I make it."

– James Baldwin

A Picture is Worth a Thousand Phone Calls

Alan Bell

BLK, Vol. 1 No. 9, August 1989

The covers of *BLK*, a US publication that billed itself as the "National Black Lesbian and Gay Newsmagazine," reflected the interests of a diverse community throughout its 41-issue run from 1988 through 1994. The inaugural edition, for instance, was dominated by an anonymous Black beefcake Santa Claus lifted off a commercial greeting card, while the fifth featured internationally renowned author and activist Audre Lorde. The idea was to hopscotch across the landscape landing in a different place each time.

A Picture is Worth a Thousand Phone Calls

For the ninth issue, seeking a man with the gravitas of Lorde, I selected James Baldwin. His life and work encapsulated the complexities of navigating multiple identities – being Black, being gay, and being an intellectual in a country rife with both prejudice and resistance to diversity. Just the sort of warrior I was looking for.

Baldwin's novels, *Giovanni's Room* and *Another Country*, groundbreaking in their candid depictions of same-sex desire, not only provided a voice for the marginalized but also erections for countless young gay men in high school. Don't ask me how I know.

Baldwin's work wasn't just a reflection of his experiences as a Black gay man but also a broader commentary on the societal norms that perpetuated exclusion and prejudice. His *Notes of a Native Son* and *The Fire Next Time* tackled race and sexuality with clarity and empathy that was far ahead of his time.

A writer with excellent credentials, who preferred to be called Ricardo Mikelson, agreed to tell Baldwin's story for *BLK*. We discussed and agreed on his approach, word count, and deadlines to accommodate an August 1989 issue date. With the heavy lifting in place, I took on the task of selecting a cover photo. Easy, right? I mean this is James Baldwin. There's got to be tons of photographs, with a good number in the public domain, right?

I made several calls, keeping notes on scraps of paper. But after those first few, it became clear that getting a photo of Baldwin wasn't going to be easy. That led to me becoming more intentional in my note-taking. The unedited narrative that follows are those notes, a kind of diary.

- Call Baldwin publisher: Bantam/ Doubleday/Dell. 212-765-XXXX.
- Bantam calls back. They don't have photo.
- Call Afro-American Museum. In a meeting will call me back later. Museum doesn't call back.

- Next day. Call museum again. They don't have photo. Suggest Afro-American Collection at A.C. Bilbrew Library.

- Call Bilbrew Library. Said they have snapshot of Baldwin, but it isn't very good, it can't circulate and if it could, they can't authorize reproduction.

- Call other libraries. Four say they have photo files, but only Santa Monica has a picture of Baldwin.

- Drive to Santa Monica. Picture turns out to be cut from magazine and therefore unacceptable for reproduction.

- Also, picture has "Santa Monica Library" stamped across the face.

- Bobby Smith (Phill Wilson's assistant) calls looking for Baldwin photos for a different project.

- Go to Different Light Bookstore to see Baldwin books. Maybe we can reproduce one already printed. Nothing useable. But note University of Massachusetts Photographic Services photo credit.

- Call Wave Publications. Say they have photo and would lend it, but want to see publication.

- Copies of *BLK* messengered over to Wave offices.

- Next day. Go to Wave to pick up photo. Thought they had one, but turns out they don't.

- Call University of Massachusetts in Boston. Told Photo Services were in Amherst.

- Call UMass in Amherst 413-545-XXXX. Donna takes order for photos. $3 a piece. Yes, she can get them out today. Will send Federal Express.

- UMass calls back. Can't send photos without authorization.

- Call *L.A. Weekly*. The head of their photo department says they don't loan photos.

- Call personal contact at *L.A. Sentinel*. Says he has one.

- Go to *Sentinel*. Can't find photo. After half hour, finally find photo, but is so closely cropped, might not be usable.

- Phill Wilson stops by. Says he has several Baldwin photos.

- Drive to Wilson's. One photo is even more closely cropped than the one from the *L.A. Sentinel*. The other is a screened velox that's too small.

- Call five bookstores in Hollywood that specialize in movie star photos. Collector's Bookstore say they have one.

- Drive to Hollywood to Collector's Bookstore. I am told that the fellow who said they had a Baldwin photo was new and had made a mistake.

- Download list of books written by Baldwin from "Books in Print" on Knowledge Index.

- Call UMass to determine permission process.

- Call St. Martin's Press. They will send if they have one. Will call back to confirm. They do not call back.

- Call New American Library. They don't have one. They suggest calling Alfred A. Knopf, 201 E. 50th St., NY. 212-751-XXXX.

- Call Knopf. They are publishing an authorized biography of Baldwin, but currently have no photos. They will fax press release about the new book, though.

- Call University of Massachusetts Press, 413-545-XXXX. (This is different from UMass Photo Service.) They have one and will send it Federal Express.

- Call Henry Holt Co., 212-633-XXXX. They don't have photo.

- Call Beverly Hills Library to locate Baldwin's agent. Told agent is Edward J. Acton Inc. (17 Grove St., NY 10014, 212-473-XXXX. Told Prentice Hall is Baldwin's major publisher.

- Call Acton. Told to call Richard Green, the lawyer for the Baldwin estate.

Encounters with James Baldwin

- Call Richard Green (212-246-XXXX). Told to write to Gloria Smart (137 W. 71st St. #1B, NY 10023), the executor of the Baldwin estate.

- Call information for Gloria Smart telephone number. Not listed.

- Call Greg Crawford, a friend who works in photo department at 20th Century Fox. He doubts that they have Baldwin photo. He confirms later that they don't.

- Call Prentice Hall at 201-592-XXXX; wrong number. Call Prentice Hall at 212-373-XXXX; wrong number. Call Prentice Hall at 212-698-XXXX. Talk to Mara. They didn't have photo, but will authorize UMass Photo Service to release photo. Mara calls back to say she can't authorize photo.

- Photo from University of Massachusetts Press arrives Federal Express. It is perfect.

Although I was pretty pissed off during the two-week process, with the photo in hand, I could be more circumspect about what I had gone through to get it. Maybe this was par for the photo-wrangling course. Whatever. I was still pissed off. But with my notes as a badge of honour and tangible record of my travels, I decided to clean them up to share and laugh with friends. Little did I know that some forty years later I'd be sharing them in this space.

I found the actual photo in a file separate from the notes. On the back, it said "JAMES BALDWIN, Photograph by Steve Long." Simultaneously I wondered who Steve Long was and if we had given him credit. We had. "Cover: James Baldwin. Story on page 13. Photo by Steve Long courtesy of University of Massachusetts Press." I googled both men and a "University of Massachusetts Amherst James Baldwin Photo Galley" came up. The *BLK* photo wasn't there but two others by Long were, with Baldwin wearing the same plaid shirt. Maybe they had retired the *BLK* photo like the number of a superstar athlete.

A Picture is Worth a Thousand Phone Calls

Looking back at the cover, I still think it's perfect. It captures the intense, serious, fierce, warrior for gay rights, for Black rights, and for human rights that was James Baldwin. I wonder what he'd think of my little odyssey. Would he be proud of my tenacity, or would he say, "Get over yourself?"

Either way, it's clear to me that part of the reason I've been able to lead the life I've led, or that I was asked to contribute to this remembrance and celebration, or that those around me have been able to do what they do, rests significantly on what James Baldwin both did and what he has come to represent.

Baldwin's enduring impact on the Black LGBTQ community is also demonstrated by how contemporary Black artists and intellectuals cite him as an influence. His fearlessness in addressing both Black and LGBTQ identities has paved the way for later generations to explore these themes in their own work. His legacy is visible in the works of modern Black writers like Jesmyn Ward, Roxane Gay, and Danez Smith, and filmmakers like Marlon Riggs, Barry Jenkins, and Ava DuVernay, all of whom continue to push boundaries and explore complex identities.

James Baldwin was a trailblazer who used his talents as a writer and his platform as a public intellectual to challenge societal norms, advocate for equal rights, and articulate the complexities of being both Black and gay. His works continue to inspire and empower, offering both a mirror and a map for navigating the challenges of identity in a diverse and often divided world.

Whether a hundred phone calls or a thousand, a little bureaucratic frustration was well worth being able to share James Arthur Baldwin with the readers of *BLK*.

Never Make Peace
with Mediocrity

Selina Brown

"You were born where you were born and faced the
future that you faced because you were Black and for
no other reason. The limits of your ambition were, thus,
expected to be set forever. You were born into a society
which spelled out with brutal clarity, and in as many
ways as possible, that you were a worthless human
being. You were not expected to aspire to excellence:
you were expected to make peace with mediocrity."

– James Baldwin, 1963, The Fire Next Time.

As a Black woman born in Birmingham, to a Black British
mother and growing up with my grandmother's strong
Jamaican influence, being Black was something I knew from
as early as I can remember. My awakening of my difference to
other children began in my reception class at school and the
anxiety I felt then is still etched in my brain. James Baldwin's
profound words, written sixty-one years ago still give me
goosebumps to this day, as they speak my truth now, as I
encounter the attitudes of those who doubt my abilities today.

This quote sums up my experiences and challenges
as I navigate the complexities of identity in UK society,
undoubtedly shaped by race. It has inspired me to achieve
more and to raise others up with me.

Education, which is supposed to be an equaliser, often
becomes a battleground where stereotypes and biases lurk
in the shadows. From being the only Black girl in my year
group at junior school, when I entered secondary school, my

classrooms were made up of predominantly white students – I felt a cultural dissonance, a lack of belonging.

On entering lecture halls and dissertation meetings, I've felt the weight of expectations and the sting of assumptions. Despite my intellect, I've had to confront the subtle yet persistent barriers hindering my academic journey. But with each hurdle, I've learned to stand taller, to assert my worth, and to demand recognition for my capabilities. I navigated the journey and became the first person in my family to attain a Master's Degree in Media Enterprise at twenty-one years old. And as I attained each success, I recalled Baldwin's words: "You were not expected to aspire to excellence: you were expected to make peace with mediocrity."

Entering the professional world of media, I've encountered a landscape marred by systemic inequalities and entrenched prejudices. Despite my qualifications and aspirations, I've faced the harsh reality of glass ceilings and closed doors. But I refuse to be defined by society's limitations. I was, and am determined to break barriers, defy stereotypes, and carve out a space where my talents are recognised and celebrated. I found peace in my travels to the motherland of Africa and my roots in Jamaica, completely different environments where being Black doesn't exist. This is where I made peace with myself.

In personal relationships and societal interactions, I've learned to navigate the complexities of identity with grace and resilience, from challenging beauty standards by cutting off my straight permed hair to wearing my natural afro with pride. By embracing my cultural heritage and learning my history, I've embraced my Blackness with pride and confidence. I've reached a stage in my life due to age and also motherhood where I refuse to conform to society's narrow definitions of beauty and worth. Instead, I celebrate the richness of my melanin, the strength of my roots, and the beauty of my diversity. For I am made in the image of my ancestors whose

DNA lives within me.

Amidst the complexities, there is an undeniable spirit of resilience that has been with me throughout my life, passed to me by my mother from her mother, and from all the great matriarchs in my family line. It is a resilience rooted in a legacy of strength, creativity, and community. It is a resilience that refuses to be silenced, diminished, or overlooked. I am not merely a survivor – I am a thriver, an architect of change, and a trailblazer in my own right.

I stand on the shoulders of the amazing Black women that shaped publishing in the UK from Mary Prince, Rosemarie Hudson, Margaret Busby, Bernardine Evaristo as well as many more. Due to their sacrifices, I was able to bring to life the largest Black Literature Festival in Europe, namely the Black British Book Festival and we staged it at the South Bank Centre in London.

The inception of the Black British Book Festival was not only about filling a void, it was about creating a space where Black authors could shine, where our stories could be heard, and where our voices can resonate with audiences eager for diverse narratives. The festival stands as a celebration of Blackness in all its forms. It is a celebration of our history, our culture, and our contributions to literature. It is a celebration of resilience in the face of adversity, a reminder that our stories matter and deserve to be told. Through panels, workshops, and author readings, the festival provides a platform for dialogue and exchange, fostering connections and amplifying voices that might otherwise go unheard.

My experiences as a Black woman in the UK have shaped my perspective and fuelled my passion for amplifying Black voices. From navigating spaces where I am often the only person of colour, to challenging stereotypes and misconceptions, my journey has been one of both struggle and triumph. But through it all, I have found strength in my identity and in the solidarity of the Black community.

For me, being Black is not merely an identity imposed upon me by society – it is a source of strength, resilience, and pride. It is a lens through which I navigate the world, forging my own path and shaping my own destiny. In the mosaic of British society, my voice and experiences are essential threads that enrich the fabric of our collective identity.

I will continue to strive to make my story a testament to the power of resilience, the beauty of diversity, and the triumph of the human spirit.

Make peace with mediocrity? … Nope, never that.

Searching for the Centennial Man

Michael Campbell

He houses an asylum of faces;
all turn on a negro carousel, while
an American calliope plays America
The Beautiful. Let him look out of
any one, head full of eyes, sleepless
as the conscience of his countrymen.

Behind the one he's now wearing,
a weary smile toils behind a rockstone
of pent-up Black lives, a balled-up
fist poised for backlash. His black lips
marshall the assembly of their voices, the
thick sprigs, cloven tongues burning,

in the light of their immolation. This fire,
is a witness to its own, reflected
in the lidless eyes of the lynch mob, in
the over-ripe stench of strange fruit;
burning without consummation, in the
planting of red-black smoke and yellow

Searching for the Centennial Man

bulbs at the feet of crosses stretching
across the South. Strange fires. This is
America postbellum, her grounded nimbuses,
her high groves of foreign gods and the
earth travailing over the issue of blood,
unholy shrines trough-deep in the offering.

But this smile, this pock-marked chin,
this skin, burnt umber/bound leather.
This bequeathing. Nose and eyes. These teeth.
This mind. This mouth. These words. This
march shall not end here, but will always
with a heart of willing flesh begin, again.

In a Photograph
with James Baldwin

Fred D'Aguiar

Left to right: Caryl Phillips, David Dabydeen, James Baldwin, Fred D'Aguiar
Photo: By permission of Fred D'Aguiar

There's a photo taken in the summer of 1986, of James Baldwin (Jimmy) just over a year before his death. I don't know who took it. My copy is black and white. There's Jimmy with Caryl Phillips, David Dabydeen, and me, in our twenties, at the Greater London Council Black Writers' Book Prizes (long defunct). There were three categories for books. David won the non-fiction prize for *Hogarth's Blacks* (1985), about the 18th-century artist who sketched ordinary street and tavern life, and other spaces of considerable depravity, and inadvertently captured Black people in London when a Black presence seemed elided. Caz won for fiction, his pristine first novel, *The Final Passage* (1985), about migration to the Mother Country from the Caribbean in the 1950s. My debut poetry collection, *Mama Dot* (1985), about growing up in the countryside of Guyana with my paternal grandmother, snagged the third category.

When I was introduced to him at the prize reception, by someone who chaired some committee or other at the GLC, I said, "Fred, great to meet you." And he said, "Jimmy; likewise." In the photo, Jimmy sports a wry smile and he's sandwiched between me and David, with Caz beside David. You can't see Jimmy's hands – where are his hands? – hidden out of sight behind our backs. I'd been nervous about meeting him. I'd read all of his books and studied his two novels, *Go Tell It on the Mountain* (1953) and *Giovanni's Room* (1956), along with two collections of his essays, *Notes of a Native Son* (1955) and *The Fire Next Time* (1963) at university. My writer-as-reader takeaway centres on the bravura of his extended sentences – akin to jazz riffs that peeled away and strayed far from their beginnings, and just as you might think them lost beyond retrieval, they drifted back on track and into sight, and onwards to new heights, and insights.

He compressed a lot of meaning into his idiosyncratically long and loping sentences. They work like an accordion: compressed to the greatest degree and then pulled apart gradually to the greatest extent to make music of endless meanings. They flower with this rhetorical flourish that belies clear argument and yet in contradictory fashion build cogent insights. I linked his athletic sentence-making to that wicked sparkle in his eyes and that broad smile that rented all the space on his head. His friendly demeanour – neither aloof nor frosty as befits an icon – put me at ease right away. In biographical terms I knew that his stepfather was a preacher and that Jimmy took to the pulpit at an early age in an apprenticeship ideally suited to voicing deep and ornate enquiry.

To return to that photograph: taken back in the day when Britain was part of Europe and Thatcherism (Stuart Hall's term) dogged Black people and the working class, you can see the clothes and big hair and glasses that function as timestamps. James Baldwin's meeting with three Black writers in Britain typified his European sojourn for the greater part of his adult life: away from America he could cast his Yeats-like cold eye on American history and contemporary culture with the merciless precision afforded by necessary distance and cool detachment. In his move to Europe (France then Switzerland) James Baldwin matched a tradition of Black Americans moving away (think of Josephine Baker, Claude McKay, Richard Wright) to preserve sanity and gain a much-needed critical perspective on America as they affirmed their humanity in another place.

The sense of the Baldwin sentence positions a first-person speaker as they regard American culture under a microscope. The aggrieved speaker charges the white-dominated society with a blind superiority that aims its hostility at Black bodies. In what appears to mirror the premise of Frantz Fanon in *Black Skin, White Masks* – that white racism damages Blacks at a psychological level which doubles down on the social costs to Blacks of second-class citizenship – Baldwin explores how Black consciousness operates with and around white impediments, in tandem with why that Black perspective appears to be preoccupied with white requirements of Blacks who wish to survive in a world of white rules. Baldwin's way in this world is an amalgam of Fanon's notion of a traumatized interiority coupled with the social codes of double consciousness as defined by Du Bois.

I looked for signs of this damage in Jimmy. After all, the baggage of trauma, as I gleaned from my early 1980s stint of training and working as a psychiatric nurse at the Maudsley, accompanies insight about the pain of consciousness of living Black under the heavy manners of a recalcitrant whiteness. Remarkably, James Baldwin's condition of a made-in-America Black psyche is compounded by the fact that he is a gay man as declared in his novel, *Giovanni's Room*. You couldn't discern pain in Jimmy's eyes, or feel it emanate from his body. He exuded confidence. He laughed with head-thrown-back abandon. His best decision may have been to leave the land of his birth and psychic torture and social upheaval as the Civil Rights movement geared up, for Europe and love and companionship, to write non-fiction, fiction and plays that emancipated a mind within the cage and pleasure dome of a Black body. It's Bob Marley's truism in 'Redemption Song': "emancipate yourself from mental slavery," taken to heart in analytical prose and emotionally charged scenes of fiction and drama.

At our meeting that evening, sluiced with a variety of fermented beverages, I asked him if he meant all those mean and admittedly funny things that he'd written about Richard Wright. (Jimmy had accused Wright of writing the white negro, in Bigger, his anti-hero protagonist in the 1940 novel, *Native Son*, that is, a version of Blackness that was chock full of rage and self-loathing and resulting violence, inculcated by white oppression.) Jimmy replied, something like, "Not mean, darling, just honest." I changed the subject by complimenting Jimmy. I told him that in his interviews (in particular, his 1963 exchange with Malcolm X and more pointedly, his 1965 debate at Cambridge University with the arch conservative William F. Buckley) and in his writings, he exhibited true wit, in the 17th-century sense of an ability to think on his feet and say something original in a memorable way. He smiled broadly and raised his eyebrows which made his big eyes even bigger (like a character from animé). I said that he balanced radicalism with flair and that he would make a model aristocrat. He said, only if he could rid the world of all the current ones.

It was the drink and the occasion talking, rather than anything serious. Our off-the-cuff remarks, not meant as evidence of any sort, seen or unseen, nevertheless warmed us to each other. He embodied that rare quality of someone who wrote as well as he talked and whose writing generated much talk. His prose enacted thinking as a process, a force, grappling with difficult and sensitive subjects. He said that my poetry affirmed place. Have I been back? Yes, I said, but when I go to Guyana, they call me English, while in the UK I'm told to go back where I came from! He laughed and said, "Welcome to the club." I wondered about the nature of that club. Was it an in-between space or a twoness that created a third condition? He asked what it was like for me to live away from my parents for so long. I said my grandmother, and the extended household of aunts and uncles and cousins and nephews, helped me to cope with the limbo of waiting to return to London where I was born. In the decade that it took for my return to become a reality, my relatives inducted me into my parents' Guyanese rhythms and outlook. Well, Jimmy said, it gave you a fine poetry book. Then some publicist whisked him away. It was the last time that I saw him. He died fifteen months later.

I value the photograph as the bequest of a literary giant of the American past, handed with confidence to the British present of my peers and I. We needed the transatlantic connection, that sense of a shared and complicit pattern to all oppression of Blacks in white-defined spaces. In keeping with John Berger's sense of the many ways to see and be seen, myriad and subjective, our look at the camera functioned as noun and verb. The male gaze quadrupled and decolonizing: looking out for each other and for ourselves all the while seemingly ready to meet any challenge. Jimmy would never be alone, no matter where he went, not if he remained in the permanent environment of this photo surrounded by three youths located in Britain and keenly aware of our history and his. He could rest easy knowing that he was being reread by writers about to embark on that troublesome journey of living to write and writing in order to live.

James Baldwin at the Albert Memorial, Kensington Gardens, London, 1969. Photo: Allan Warren

Fires In Our Time

Thomas Glave

"Remember our history and never forget it," James Baldwin would insist if he were with us right now. Either on page after fiery page, or out loud with that gravelly preacher's voice, he'd tell us that indifference to history (and to the ongoing cruelty of human suffering and annihilation), is a cheap luxury nobody can afford. He would tell us that a brown-skinned South Asian British Tory prime minister can be as inhuman as his white "hostile environment" predecessors. Recalling British history we shouldn't be surprised, Baldwin would say, that the British government planned to round up and deport some of the most vulnerable and traumatized people on the planet – human beings seeking asylum – to unknown and potentially dire fates in Rwanda. "Because look at the atrocities that the British committed throughout the entire range and length of their Empire," I can hear him shouting. "They sold, murdered, raped, pillaged, flayed, tortured, dismembered, castrated, lynched, bombed, segregated, named other people's lands after their invading men, named people's *countries* according to their own whims and designs, and did much more through the raging fires of those times that is yet to be revealed. So why should anyone be astonished now, after the arrogance and xenophobia of Brexit and the Brexiteers, that Britain's government is returning to its habitual cruelty?"

Baldwin's words remind us that time and time again, history has shown us exactly who these Empire-minded people are, who they have always been, who they've hated through the centuries, and what they continually aim to do with that well-nourished hatred lying just beneath their mellifluous accents and delusions of greatness.

History: *Recollect. Remember.*

Remember that not so far from the UK, another fire in our time rages through the Israeli army's ongoing genocide against Palestinians. In this one hundredth year since Baldwin's birth, the question of whose land is actually whose will never be solved by bombing and burning innocent civilians, including infants and children, bringing survivors red-tinged dreams. As dreams of genocide are always red, so Baldwin's words slashing through the atrocities remain fiercely black and white, exhorting all of us to *do* something – do whatever we can to protest this horror, one of several in our time. To call attention to it and deplore its perpetrators, as we confront those who insist that any criticism of Israel, and specifically criticism of its current and past brutality towards Palestinians, is unquestionably anti-Semitism.

History: *Recollection.*

Recollecting that just about everything that Baldwin wrote through the landscapes of fighting for social justice and civil rights prepared us for the fact that right now innumerable women in the United States are contending with two histories that have long existed in bitter relation to each other: the time when a woman possessed absolutely no right to decide what to do with her body and an undesired pregnancy (and could be imprisoned or worse for risking an illegal action on her own behalf), and the not-long-ago era when those anti-abortion draconian laws were overturned by the US Supreme Court, up until when that august institution, in 2023 unfortunately controlled by a super-majority of politically conservative white men, decided to return the United States to the time of woman-as-less-than, woman as subordinate, woman as "Have my baby, bitch, even if I rape you, and *deal* with it."

Baldwin would implore us to understand that these new

restrictions placed upon a woman's right to choose will have a greater impact upon the lives of poor women and working-class women, including innumerable women of colour. If we keep tight hold of historical memory, can we not once again feel the hot breath of the plantations on all our necks, and the gruesome crackling fires of those "your-body-belongs-to-*me*" times never very far away?

The year of Baldwin's birth was an intensely incendiary time of Jim Crow laws, segregation, voting poll taxes, Ku Klux Klan nighttime hot crosses, sharecropping, lynchings, forced displacements, and more. He never forgot any of it and made it his life's great work to remember and retell it all. Nine years later, in 1933, across the sea, Dachau would open quietly, without the blaring of foreboding trumpets. God was giving few people, if any, the promising rainbow sign back then. The year of Baldwin's birth and the years that followed still look and sound far too much like our present fiery time, as we see in the blood libel and fascism from the mouth of a US demagogue who speaks of immigrants "infecting the blood of our country." The same demagogue who refers to Haiti and other Black nations as "shithole countries," who refers to Mexicans as "rapists," and who brags about grabbing women by their genitalia. Trump's followers love him, worship him, as the followers of Hitler, Mussolini, and Stalin loved and worshipped them. In our time a demagogue's followers have kindled bright torches and marched in dark hours across a university's campus, shouting in hateful rage that they will not be "replaced" by Jews or any *others*.

Yet every blazing word that Baldwin wrote warned us and will warn those yet to come, if we all survive the increasing fires of our warming planet, that such worship – the cheering of cruelty and suffering – can never be a viable human option. In essays, plays and novels, he challenged the United States to be a better country – the country of his birth that he both despised and loved, the country that most definitely never learnt to love him back. Through all those books and reflections that are our inheritance, he witnessed too that the France he came to love felt no love for Algerians – they especially despised strangers in the village – and no love for "French" West Africans either. No love for Vietnamese people or Sri Lankans, and certainly no love for its citizens from the Caribbean *départements d'outre-mer*, our diasporic cousins.

History: *Remembrance.*

And so in this one hundredth year since your birth, welcome to 2024, Mr Baldwin. The fires of your time continue to snarl through the flames of our own, burning and scorching well into the future, decimating our planet, albeit with some – and sometimes many – rainbow colours. As we stride toward the fires and battle through them, supporters of Black Lives Matter worldwide reflect on your prescient words in *No Name in the Street*, progressive hip-hoppers recall your words in *Notes of a Native Son,* and if we're brave enough to read your story 'Going to Meet the Man' and face the tale's terror and vaulting beauty, lively conversations inevitably spring up.

Now is the time when the writer-preacher-prophet's voice still admonishes through dreams of all colours, impelling us and all who listen ever closer to a breathable future and the evidence of our freedom that must be freedom for everyone, still not clearly seen.

Can I get an Amen, Somebody?

Sonia Grant

"The church was very exciting. It took a long time for me to disengage myself from this excitement, and on the blindest, most visceral level, I never really have, and never will. There is no music like that music, or drama like the drama of the saints rejoicing, the sinners moaning, the tambourines racing, and all those voices coming together and crying holy unto the Lord. There is still, for me, no pathos quite like the pathos of those multi-coloured, worn, somehow triumphant and transfigured faces, speaking from the depths of a visible, tangible, continuing despair of the goodness of the Lord."

– James Baldwin, *The Fire Next Time*[1]

By his own admission, James Baldwin was a lapsed Pentecostalist and whilst he may have physically left the church, its imprint was an indelible one. More than bricks and mortar, the church was a set of rigid rules and regulations that shaped his character and perspective, especially in terms of his lifelong quest to make sense of a world contorted by racism, discrimination, and injustice. Although he had many legitimate issues with the church, inadvertently, it lit a rage within him that was never really extinguished. Arguably, Baldwin's sense of social justice began percolating from the time he emerged as a boy preacher, aged fourteen to seventeen, when he made his escape from the church's strictures that had begun to

---

1 James Baldwin, *The Fire Next Time*, New York: Dial Press, 1963, p. 47.

suffocate him and before it thwarted his burgeoning ambition to express himself through writing.

My introduction to James Baldwin's writing was in 1987, courtesy of the Lyric Theatre's production of his first play, *The Amen Corner*. I took my chance and skipped a youth meeting and headed to Shaftesbury Avenue, London, not only to support a friend who was singing in the choir but, importantly, news had circulated that James Baldwin had been invited to London and there was every possibility he might be in the audience.

The late 1980s was an era in which, as a person of colour, I felt invisible. Whether it was film, TV or the theatre, there seemed little, if any, representation of people who looked like me – until *The Amen Corner* was staged. Indeed, Baldwin stated as early as 1969, that "Black people ignored the theatre because the theatre had always ignored them."[2]

The play had already had a successful run at The Tricycle Theatre[3] in London, and was being transferred to the West End. It signified a series of 'firsts'. In addition to its all-Black cast (with Carmen Monroe in the lead role as Sister Margaret), it had a Black director (Anton Phillips) and it was produced by a Black theatre company (Carib Theatre Productions).

I was exhilarated. Coming from Luton, a dull, industrial town that seemed like a cultural wilderness, my only exposure to theatre up to that point had been going on my mother's work outings to see pantomime at Christmas. However, in my youth, I secretly yearned to write, but didn't have the wherewithal. Moreover, I convinced myself that it was the preserve of white, middle class people, and not for someone who looked like me. While I didn't come from a background

---

2 James Baldwin, 'Sweet Lorraine,' (1969) in *To Be Young, Gifted and Black: Lorraine Hansberry in Her Own Words* adapted by Robert Nemiroff, New York: Vintage Books, 1995, p 18.

3 Now known as Kiln Theatre.

of abject poverty like Baldwin, retrospectively, I now realise that there was a pernicious culture, one of low expectations at my school. The trajectory for boys was that they were headed straight for the assembly line at Vauxhall Motors, which was considered very well-paid and, at the time, a job for life. The girls tended to go into secretarial work or, those lucky enough, became clerical assistants in the Civil Service. I do remember that several friends were contemplating nursing; one, however, was put off because she was offered training as a State Enrolled Nurse (SEN), despite having the qualifications to become a higher-ranking State Registered Nurse (SRN). When I asked her why she wasn't applying she replied: "Emptying bedpans is not my thing." As far as Baldwin was concerned, if he didn't flee to Paris, America's discrimination and segregation dictated a lifetime of menial jobs.

Every young person deserves an Orilla Winfield in their lives, as Baldwin had. His grade school teacher showed not only great kindness towards the gifted youngster, but she introduced him to a world of culture and possibilities, encouraging Baldwin to write his first play at the age of eleven.

As an adult, I pursued journalism as a career, and when I actively sought out creative writing opportunities, I was advised to "write what you know." In that respect, I was inspired by the authenticity of Baldwin's portrayals in *The Amen Corner*.

There were similarities between Baldwin's 'church' experience, described as the holiness tradition i.e. Pentecostalism, and my own background, which is why the play resonated. Certain preachers seldom strayed beyond the Old Testament. "Turn with me to…" the preacher would begin assuredly and, as cheeky young people, we always finished the sentence under our breath "… the Book of Revelation." Invariably, emphasis was placed on "hell fire and brimstone" and the avoidance of sinning.

Encounters with James Baldwin

The regime was unforgiving: Church attendance was mandatory two or three times during the week for prayer meeting, bible study, or choir rehearsal. Most Saturdays involved being driven up and down the country in a barely roadworthy Bedford van, and transported from one meeting to the next, where we saw the same old faces; and on Sundays – morning glory, Sunday school and evening service. And, if you were absent without leave (AWOL), a church "mother" would demand a satisfactory explanation. So, as strange as it may seem, missing a youth meeting when I was a teenager to go and see *The Amen Corner* was viewed as an act of rebellion.

Baldwin began writing *The Amen Corner* in 1952. However, his obstinacy was already evident, as the delay in the play's first production wasn't because he'd incubated the work, rather it was partly due to the fact that he "did not want to enter the theatre on the theatre's terms but on [his own]."[4] Moreover, Baldwin was anxious and unsure if the play would work: "Writing *The Amen Corner,* I remember as a desperate and even rather irresponsible act – it was certainly considered irresponsible by my agent at that time. She did not wish to discourage me, but it was her duty to let me know that the American theatre was not exactly clamouring for plays on obscure aspects of Negro life,"[5] he wrote. Even though Baldwin and his agent may have had reservations regarding the merits of a play depicting a specific demographic, what subsequently transpired illustrated the extent to which fate or good fortune played in its eventual staging.

According to David Leeming in *James Baldwin: A Biography,* "Owen Dodson, a writer and the director of the Howard University Players in Washington D.C., was looking […] for a play by a Black playwright." The timing couldn't have been better: Baldwin desperately wanted an audience for his play, one in which he had confidence but, nevertheless, "had

---

4 James Baldwin, *The Amen Corner*, New York: Dial Press, 1968, 'Notes of The Amen Corner', p. 17.

5 *Ibid*, xi.

been trying without success to sell the idea of a professional production of *The Amen Corner"* but was resigned to the fact that "there was 'no market' for a play about a storefront church in Harlem." Apparently, a friend of Dodson's told him about the play and he contacted Baldwin. Dodson's specificity meant that the play was a perfect fit and would be performed by the Howard University Players. Although it was an amateur outfit it had earned a professional reputation, and the fact that Howard University was a leading member of the Historically Black University and College (HBCU) network wouldn't have been lost on Baldwin.

In the play, Sister Margaret's authority ebbed away, as parishioners became emboldened to challenge her hypocrisy. Similarly, when most of my peers began to drift away from the church, they reasoned that the church leaders were unrelatable. The strictures of Pentecostalism meant many were ill-prepared for the world outside. On the "forbidden" list for girls were make-up, jewellery, wearing trousers or going to the cinema. Consequently, many of my friends mastered the art of code-switching. Either consciously or unconsciously they'd change their accent, tone, mannerisms or demeanour, depending on their situations or surroundings in order to "fit in."

In that regard, we identified with the character of David and his "pain". He was the personification of many youths who yearned to escape the church's vice-like grip. While Sister Margaret feared that David would be swallowed up by the vices of a secular music industry, our church "mothers" feared that our young men would be subjected to police 'Stop and Search' (SUS) and criminalised by the legal system. Gradually, however, young people at my church began imperceptibly to inch their way to the exit door. In my case, a six-month internship to work for a United Nations NGO in New York severed the tie in one fell swoop.

As soon as I arrived, I knew that visiting Harlem would

be a priority. I had every intention of visiting Baldwin's old store front church, the Fireside Pentecostal Church. I sought out a relative who lived in Harlem – my glamour-puss great aunt, Amy, who, every time I visited, could be found posing on her chaise longue like Eartha Kitt. When I told her my plans, she was horrified and scared for me. In her estimation, I lacked street-smarts. She suggested I visit the Abyssinian Baptist Church instead – its former leader was the controversial and charismatic preacher and congressman Adam Clayton Powell Jr – whom she felt would be more "appropriate". When I visited, the balcony was filled with tourists out for what I referred to as their Blues Brothers' fix: namely "holy rolling" which means dancing, shaking and other boisterous movements by church attendees who perceive themselves as being under the influence of the Holy Spirit. It seemed to me that's all the tourists really came to see and experience. Indeed, after the choir's rousing renditions, the preacher, an erudite "Morehouse Man", approached the lectern. The visitors, however, were not interested in a sermon, as they all got up and left.

In reading reviews of *The Amen Corner* over the years, it was noticeable that reviewers didn't stray much beyond the play's "sweet gospel music". Conceivably, it was an indicator that they weren't particularly interested in critiquing the nuances of the Black church. Rather, a prevailing sentiment of British reviewers was that it "was too long and would benefit from some judicious editing." *The Guardian* theatre critic Michael Billington, referring to a 2013 London performance wrote, "I don't think *The Amen Corner* is a great play, but I get the feeling it is one that its author, James Baldwin, was compelled to write."

In my own writing, I have concentrated on non-fiction – social justice issues, in particular – and haven't yet felt a compulsion to mine my formative church years, but I take as my cue the previous encouragement to "write what I know" and am tempted. As it happens, my paternal grandmother,

Can I get an Amen, Somebody?

Clothilda, was a pastor and preacher in Jamaica. Unfortunately, I never met her, so if I do write something, it will probably be a piece of creative non-fiction. By most accounts, Clothilda seems to have ruled with an iron fist or "the rod of correction", as she dispensed her particular brand of religion.

In a foreword to *The Amen Corner,* speaking of Sister Margaret, Baldwin wrote, "She is in the church because her societies left her no other place to go." This has led me to reconsider, especially commemorating Windrush75, perhaps penning a dramatic piece (I do like the immediacy of the theatre) to pay homage to my Pentecostal upbringing, although I am now non-denominational. One of the founding members of my former church was a lady who was a passenger on the *HMT Empire Windrush.* She started the church in her living room, with prayer meetings for a handful of like-minded people. This was because she had attended a local Methodist church and, when the service ended, the pastor shook her hand, thanked her for coming, but told her in so many words: "Please don't come back next Sunday." I've gained a fresh insight into the plight of matriarchal West Indian church leaders. Their attempts to batten down the hatches and thus keep a hostile world at bay, was not dissimilar to the ways of Sister Margaret.

American critics attempted to write off Baldwin, an iconoclastic writer, who had excoriated America for decades, with the charge that he was living in exile, out of touch, and that his influence was waning. The overwhelming response to the London production of the play, however, suggested otherwise. I was gutted that James Baldwin hadn't been in the audience on the evening I attended but, nonetheless, was pleased that he mustered the energy to travel from the South of France to London at Anton Phillips' invitation. By then, Baldwin, who was always a slightly-built man, was extremely gaunt and his body had been ravaged by the cancer to which he would eventually succumb. Visiting the show turned out to be one of Baldwin's last public appearances.

Baldwin once said that he left the church to become a writer but "never left the pulpit." His religious upbringing cast a long shadow, as was apparent from the titles of some of his works, among them: *Go Tell It on the Mountain, The Devil Finds Work*, and *The Amen Corner*. The breadth of Baldwin's work illustrates for me personally that his prophetic "voice" is as relevant today as it was then.

What Kind Of World Is This?

Zita Holbourne

What kind of world is this where those supposed to uphold the law

Break it with impunity, take lives like they matter no more

Empowered by institutions, stained with the blood of Black women and men

Unwavering in their hatred even when taking the lives of children

What kind of world is this where 'Black Lives Matter' is a hashtag

Where a trip to the shop could end in a body bag

Where 'hands up don't shoot' is a protest slogan

Held up in response to Black lives stolen

What kind of world is this where the systemic denigration

Oppression, race and sex discrimination

Pervading every element of life and society

Denies the right in life to dignity and equity

But is also structured to protect the perpetrators

When lives are brutally taken, appointing infiltrators

To obstruct the course of justice, distorting truths as they spy

On families too tortured by their quest for truth to even cry?

What Kind of World is This?

The Inspirational Blues

Paterson Joseph

When I went to audition for *Blues for Mister Charlie* at the Royal Exchange Theatre in Manchester in late 1992, I wasn't really aware of James Baldwin or his writing.

Having spent the two previous years of my acting life at the Royal Shakespeare Company (RSC) and the Royal National Theatre (RNT), I was becoming tired of the standard repertoire of classical European plays. To make matters worse, I followed this marathon of Shakespeare with many months on stage at the RNT in George Farquhar's late restoration period comedy, *The Recruiting Officer*. I knew I was privileged to perform great works with great practitioners at exalted institutions and I did not take that lightly. But there remained this feeling of a hollowness in it all that I could not escape.

The Recruiting Officer has a hard centre despite its more frivolous exterior of comic artisans and upper-class procrastinating fools. It speaks of the ruling class's venality and shallow manipulations while recruiting peasants, that is the working class, to fight a war that, if it were to prove victorious for the country, would have little or no effect on their tough, rural life. There are, undoubtedly, depths to be plumbed in this play. However, the toy-town stage set and the production in general left me feeling unreal in an unreal world. It was the first and last existential, artistic crisis of my early career. My urgent, persistent question: What is it all for?

I had come into the profession without any knowledge of theatre history or tradition but imbibed much depth and purpose from the writings of Konstantin Stanislavski, Peter

Brook and Jerzy Grotowski. I believed before the RSC/ RNT period that theatre was a potentially powerful catalyst for social commentary and even change. Working with Cheek by Jowl Theatre Company, led by Declan Donnellan, had reinforced this idea in my mind when in the spring of 1990 we took our shows, *The Tempest* and *Philoctetes,* on a world tour. The highlights of this trip were the performances we gave at the national theatres of Romania and the country then known as Czechoslovakia. Witnessing students screaming "Freedom" from the balconies down onto the heads of the people, (mostly men) seated in the front rows of the stalls, stopping the show on those nights, was an unforgettable demonstration of the power I believed theatre held. The artists who took the reins of power in the revolutions that rose up later that year were colleagues, fellow travellers, who we enjoyed meeting in private spaces as they discussed the issues and solutions they were wrestling with at that time. Theatre as a catalyst for change writ large.

Yet, two years later, in 1992, after gratefully ending the run of *The Recruiting Officer* at the RNT, I was sure that theatre had lost its meaning for me – two years and more of classical European theatre and the oftentimes complacent audiences it attracted had done nothing to encourage a more positive view.

Enter Artistic Director of the Royal Exchange Theatre in Manchester, Greg Hersov. Greg had been raised in apartheid South Africa and was deeply conscious of the need for purposeful theatre. He had insisted, when interrogated by a frustrated and already jaded, young Black British actor about why he wanted to do this play, that he'd desired to direct James Baldwin's *Blues for Mister Charlie* since he had first read the playtext as a teenager. Greg's sincerity and humility were affecting – and despite my sense of theatre burnout – I found his sincere desperation to fulfil that teenage dream refreshing and even inspirational. I hoped the experience would prove as fulfilling as the promise of that meeting.

Blues for Mister Charlie is James Baldwin's response to a moment of American tragedy. He did not really know if theatre, a medium he'd only dabbled in, was the right place to discuss the issues of racism in America. As he writes in the preface to the 1964 edition of the play:

> "I did not then [in 1958], and don't now, have much respect for what goes on in the American Theatre. I am not convinced that it is a Theatre; it seems to me a series, merely, of commercial speculations, stale, repetitious, and timid."

This seemed to reflect my post-RNT feelings about British Theatre. Baldwin, in his preface, goes on to say:

> "[*Blues for Mister Charlie*] is based, very distantly indeed, on the case of Emmett Till – the Negro youth who was murdered in Mississippi in 1955 […] I do not know why the case pressed on my mind so hard – but it would not let me go […] The play then, for me, takes place in Plaguetown, U.S.A., now. The plague is race, the plague is our concept of Christianity: and this raging plague has the power to destroy every human relationship […] We are walking in terrible darkness here, and this is one man's attempt to bear witness to the reality and the power of light."

Blues for Mister Charlie begins with the murder of a young Black man, Richard Henry, who having spent years seeking his musical fortune in the north of the country – becoming burnt out on drugs and the high life – returns to the southern town where he was raised and where his widowed father, Meridian, a preacher, still lives. Richard is no longer 'fit' for the deference southern whites expect of its Black citizens. His inevitable, violent confrontation with Lyle Britten, the town's leading racist, leads to his tragic murder. The rest of the play is a series of flashes back and forth, culminating in the final act's courtroom scenes. Baldwin brilliantly affords us many insights into the tropes of white supremacist thinking and the struggles for freedom amongst America's Black populace.

James Baldwin attempts to write in a balanced, honest way

without easy, two-dimensional portrayals of the mindset of the racist white citizens and the compromised ones, too. We see this struggle as it is manifested, in the person of liberal-leaning white newspaperman, Parnell James. Parnell is an archetype of the white man in the middle. He sees, loves and knows intimately, both communities. However, in the final courtroom scene he cannot bring himself to side with the truth that the Black citizens all know – that they are denied true freedom and true, impartial justice. Inevitably, despite the odd glimmer of hope that it might be otherwise, an all-white, all-male jury acquit Lyle Britten of the murder of Richard Henry.

We are forced to note the insanity and ignorance of racism, the implications of encouraging white supremacy, particularly amongst the inarticulate, white working class, and that false notion of superiority inevitably leading to violent conclusions. The internal and external struggles of each protagonist are clearly and fairly drawn. This is not a play of easy villains and easy victims; both are compromised and blind in their own ways. We observe the consequences of the notion of 'White American Exceptionalism', a kind of divine right to rule, and the painful, righteous, and powerful resistance of the Black populace to that lie – two great forces that are in a locked battle for survival even today.

In particular, among the Black characters, we have strong female protagonists, women who have their voices heard, unusually for the early 1960s, a time of restrictive gender roles. Juanita, a conscious and vocal young activist is the object of men's desires, but she is no 'object', rather she is a force for change and Black female autonomy. Juanita speaks for herself, and her pain is that she cannot help the men she loves see their way out of their fatal, futile flaws. Mother Henry, Richard's grandmother, cares with a lioness's heart for her men, father and son, and in court verbalises the realities and frustrations of Black matriarchs in the struggle for full citizenship:

Encounters with James Baldwin

"No white man never called my husband Mister, neither, not as long as he lived. Ain't no white man called **me** *Mrs. Henry before today. I had to get a grandson killed for that."* And of the white authorities she declares to a young activist, *"I used to hate them, too, son. But I don't hate them no more. They too pitiful."*

In *Blues for Mister Charlie* the female protagonists are not tokenistic, background figures but vital players in the wider battle against oppression of white against Black. The idea that Black men are impotent in the face of racist authorities who have absolute power over their bodies and liberty, is off-set by the sense that the energy of true, forceful and lasting change will almost certainly be mediated through the female spirit; deceased mother, young woman and grandmother. It is they who will play a major role in carving a space out for themselves and their people.

*

Researching the world of *Blues for Mister Charlie* led me to read more extensively on Black consciousness. The authors I found then were my earliest teachers on a subject that had been the background noise of my life. I had no one in my life, up to that point in my early twenties, who talked of these things with any great depth. Plenty of passion but not a lot of wide-ranging knowledge – even the most basic knowledge as to where to seek and find this material. Now, I met two supreme proponents of theories on Black consciousness, namely Aimé Césaire, father of the Négritude movement that swept through Francophone literature,[1] and his fellow Martinican, Frantz Fanon.

Baldwin mirrors Césaire's take on the violent consequences of racism as it is manifested in a colonised setting, and how interconnected all oppressed peoples are:

"In the whole world, no poor devil is lynched, no wretch is

---

1   Sisters Jeanne and Pauline Nardal were also originators of the Négritude movement.

tortured, in whom I too am not degraded and murdered."[2]

In many ways Frantz Fanon, a former pupil of Césaire, has a stronger take on American racial oppression:

"Two centuries ago, a former European colony decided to catch up with Europe. It succeeded so well that the United States of America became a monster, in which the taints, the sickness and the inhumanity of Europe have grown to appalling dimensions."[3]

I read Malcolm X for the first time and Martin Luther King Jr in greater detail. I was plugging in to centuries of Black Thought and it changed me forever. Through this play, James Baldwin awoke in me a sense that I had, up until then, given only passing thought. The sense that while I am an artist first, I am a Black artist by default. In the final analysis, I slowly grew in confidence that my ethnicity, while not all of me, was as vital a part of me as my artistic sensibilities.

I mused at the time that Baldwin was such a broad and profound thinker and writer, that if the civil rights imperative had not been the engine that drove much of his work, he would have been 'free' to write more widely still. I have since, of course, realised as Césaire has it, that for some of us, poetry is the only solution to the immense despair that reigns among us. In the face of the injustices of racism and white supremacy we have a profound duty as artists. When we note oppression, wherever it may be, whether it applies directly to our given circumstances or to another's, we, as artists, must act against that oppression in the only way we know how: creatively and directly.

The compulsion to speak out when voices had been silenced, the compulsion that I sensed in Baldwin's work, had already been in mine since I was eighteen years old and could be seen in my early writings. Work that I shyly hid in my bottom drawer at home. I was, after all, ESN, educationally

2 Aimé Césaire, *Et les chiens se taisaient*, quoted in *Black Skin, White Masks* by Frantz Fanon, Pluto Press, 1986, p. 83.
3 Frantz Fanon, *The Wretched of the Earth,* Grove Press, 1961.

subnormal, according to the UK educational system I grew up with during the 1960s and 1970s. My hidden work was always about the conditions of my people, African Caribbean Black people who were struggling to be acknowledged as full citizens in many arenas – some of us struggling to even know where we belonged. Being left out of our textbooks and mainstream media was a form of silent but powerful erasure and oppression. That oppression was subtle but profound, silencing our voices and denying us our part in world history – except, of course, as it pertained to the white European colonial project. Savages who became slaves who had now become 'issues' and 'problems'. How to articulate the rage and frustration this elicited was mysterious to me. I thought perhaps I needed to merely do 'the work'. Act. Be excellent. Let my talent speak for my humanity.

Yet here was James Baldwin, proving to me without a shadow of a doubt that no matter how compromised we all are in the context of an oppressed and silenced minority, we could still live freely enough to express that resistance in artistic forms. Our remit was far from being narrow and irrelevant to world history, it was expansive and essential. It might even improve not only our own lives and mental health but, at its best, inspire a new Black British generation to feel their sense of belonging as a casual, obvious and observable, quantifiable, and undeniable truth. Another by-product of this 'speaking out', we hoped, might be that there would be more routes to artistic expression for this upcoming generation, and that their choices and access to forms of that creative expression might be broadened by the work we did in this arena. We hoped for too much, of course, but then the ideal is nearly always just out of reach when it comes to art.

In *Blues for Mister Charlie,* likewise, Baldwin feared he had hoped too much that change might come from these expressions of theatrical power. He wrote in the preface to the play:

The Inspirational Blues

"I certainly didn't see much future for me in that framework, and I was profoundly unwilling to risk my morale and my talent – my life – in endeavours which could only increase a level of frustration already dangerously high."

Blues for Mister Charlie ends with a courtroom scene. In Manchester in 1992, where the play was being staged, I could see the profound divide that existed in that major English city. Black people were seldom to be seen either walking into or working in the city centre. I noted that in the outlying areas of Hume, Longsight, and Moss Side, many global majority communities lived and worked. The African Caribbean communities still make up the majority of its residents. These areas were largely run-down and under-represented, or not represented at all, in their local councils and civic institutions. However, in a post-performance town-hall-style session, many faces signified that the ethnic mix in the Royal Exchange audience was unusually eclectic that evening.

After the Black residents of Manchester had spoken of police oppression, disproportionate incarceration and unemployment, racist housing authorities as well as local estate agents and their purposeful 'distillation' of Black and brown peoples into pockets 'more suited' to them, an elderly white man rose up and declared that he had been profoundly affected by what he had heard that night from the Black residents of Manchester. He confessed that whenever he had heard of racist treatment by the law enforcement authorities, he had dismissed these complaints as largely unfounded and irrationally paranoid. This man was typical of the usual audience member in that theatre, but that night he had to admit that he had previously been wrong to dismiss the claims of institutional racism made by the Black people of Manchester. He apologised for his former cynicism and promised to listen with more empathy in the future – a small, and to some, unimportant moment of one man's enlightenment. For me, there was a sense that while we would not cause the tide of traditional and endemic segregation and oppression of the Black populace to be finally dissipated, there were people who could be educated for the better.

Art is a catalyst for change when it is delivered with balanced, thoughtful, powerful and direct truth. Baldwin was the catalyst for that change in many, and he gave strength to the Black members of that audience. Manchester has changed in those thirty-odd years and the city centre is now much more representative of the true demographic of Greater Manchester and surrounding areas.

Sadly, Baldwin never wrote for the theatre again. *The Amen Corner,* written a decade before *Blues for Mister Charlie* was his only other venture into this particular form of artistic expression. Yet, if I could talk to him today, I would tell him that the work he did in the theatre had a profound effect on many artists, thousands of miles away on the other side of the Atlantic Ocean, and decades after he laid down his reluctant, theatrical ambitions. For the risks he took with his personal and artistic soul, and where his play led me, I will be forever grateful.

Letter to My Daughter

Peter Kalu

Dear Naomi,

I have composed versions of this letter while walking along Manchester's Curry Mile, while lying on the floor of my friend's living room in the early morning, and while driving through pouring rain to Glasgow at night. I hope the version I'm typing now makes it out – fourth time lucky!

Me and you are separated in age by forty years. I'm separated from civil rights activist, James Baldwin by forty years too, so I sit at the midpoint in the timeline stretching from James Baldwin to you; the rather quirky image that comes to mind is that of a butterfly – with the first wing being James Baldwin and the second wing being yourself. I'm in the middle trying to connect wing to wing so this letter can fly!

I was born in Manchester, England, in the 1960s when Baldwin was writing his Harlem essays. At that time in America, court-sanctioned racial segregation – of buses and restaurants and washrooms among many other places – still existed. Meanwhile, in England in 1968, the notorious Conservative MP, Enoch Powell (you can look up Powell's Wiki for his trajectory from prodigy to false prophet[9]) made his scaremongering, "Rivers of Blood" speech about the dread prospect of having a Black neighbour who preferred eating rice over potatoes: "I am filled with foreboding; like the Roman, I seem to see the River Tiber 'foaming with much blood,'" he declared; all was doom if significant immigration

8 https://en.wikipedia.org/wiki/Enoch_Powell

from Britain's former colonies was allowed to continue. Powell's speech went the 1960s equivalent of *viral* – and England promptly entered into a fever about 'race relations.'

What do I remember of it? A memory floats up from my childhood which I haven't ever spoken about to others so it's uncontaminated by the process of telling and retelling. I'm five, and I'm toddling alongside my Danish mother down Burton Road. My mother is unhappy, her jaw clenched; she's pushing my little sister in the pram. We've been in and out of some shops. She's bought sausages and lard from the butcher's shop, and the butcher said something that upset her; she's crying now as she bumps the pram up a kerb onto the pavement. We reach a public bench by a junction near the hospital road. Three powdered older ladies wearing scarves are sitting there. They see us and ask to stroke the curls of my hair. Mum lets them. As they stroke, they say, "So beautiful, so beautiful." My mum bursts into tears – tears of release, of happiness.

Looking back, I consider that of course my mother had absorbed racist stereotypes by the time she started dating my Nigerian dad because nobody escapes them – race-waters run so deep. But when your children are born, the shock-love that this engenders – the devotion to these living wonders you've given birth to – overflows stereotype: you want your children to grow freely and fully, unconstrained by the reduction that is 'racialism' as the term was in those days. Yet, pushing that pram along Burton Road, the open jibes such as those she suffered at the butcher's shop, the snide, *sotto voce* remarks, faces slipping into momentary disgust, must have brought on confusion in my mum, then anger. Because society was whispering incessantly, "your children can never be full, your children can never be normal, they are half-citizens, only half-white. Walk among us but walk with shame."

So, we reach the three powdered ladies on the bench. And yes, to stroke a Black child's hair and marvel at it, is 'othering'.

But, back then, it was everything my mother needed. My five-year-old self knew then only that it made her happy. Now, looking back, I can see she wanted to swing down the high street, proud of her brood, saying, "Look what wonders we brought into the world!" Instead, she walked with tears and hunched shoulders past Kenilworth and Walsingham Avenues. And afterwards, back inside the house, a Danish swear word was delivered to the walls, before turning to the pile of clothes in the wash tub.

The memory I'm describing is like a black and white Super 8mm cinefilm, spooling jerkily, a sad film that ends in tears and swearing. Yet change was happening, back then, thanks to those in the 1960s like my mother and father who resisted privately by their daily acts, and thanks to those public figures such as James Baldwin who led public protest and resistance. I didn't know of Baldwin back then, but there were other Black inspirations – such as Muhammad Ali and Malcolm X – of a more incendiary disposition even than Baldwin, who seeped into our home, whether through the black and white TV in our living room, or carried in conversation between my mother or father, or in other, unexpected ways. I never learned who named the family cat Stokely Carmichael, but she got the revolutionary message her name brought her, and was a card-carrying revolutionary to me.

Stokely was cool as hell. Every morning, she sauntered into the rose bushes of our racist neighbour's garden and took a shit there. In the late evening, she would sit on the fence and caterwaul at those stuck-up people and their snow-white dog that they loved to set on us. The neighbours threw buckets of water at Stokely. Curses. Occasionally, they aimed stones. Stokely dodged everything and slinked off, as impervious and immortal as a pharaoh (a memory leaps up unbidden: when she was killed by a car on the main road, she was buried with full ceremonies in our front garden, but let's skip back to Stokely in her prime). One summer afternoon, the American Stokely appeared on our snow-globe cathode-ray television. Both me and the cat Stokely sat and watched, rapt, as Carmichael took to the mic and threw off his jacket. He said, "Black Power!" and "We ain't going nowhere!" to an audience of loving Black people who were all shiny-faced, their chins high, lips firm, hair pricked, and clapping him to the rafters. "Tell it! Tell it!" He wasn't done. He told on. "Not one of those reporters here in this room is Black and they calling me the racist!" Stokely sticking it to the white man! We loved it. Telling it straight to that fine, fine Black audience. "The world belongs to you!" "No more unpunished murders!", "Be proud of your Black brothers and sisters rebelling!" Watching Stokely Carmichael, that white-shirted, black-skinned, shiny-faced truth-sayer, I felt pride growing in every cell of my being. "Black Power!" I shouted, marching around the living room, with cat Stokely following. "Black Power!" "We ain't going nowhere!" Me and Stokely strutted extra cool that week.

Compared with the 1960s, things have gotten better. OK, Black female backing singers are still wrapping warmth round the cold-white-male voices of pop stars, but much less frequently now. Black men are still keeping their pitch up – holding off the bass in their voice – in white-dominated workplaces, in order to suggest amiability and seem less threatening; and Black women are still under pressure to lower their pitch in white workplaces, speaking in. a. way. that. suggests. calm. and. ease… to diffuse the enduring stereotype of the aggressive Black female. It contorts us continuing to have to adjust like this for white people, and it contorts white people too.

Can I introduce a horse here? Horses make a landscape look more beautiful, said Alice Walker (it's the title of one of her poetry collections). Horses do that for letters too. This letter's horse is called Stereotypes. The cultural theorist, Stuart Hall rides hard on them. He says there's no escape from racial stereotypes, they are too deeply coded in the language and culture. So how to deal with them? Hall identifies "reversing the stereotype" (i.e. embracing the stereotype put forward by white discourse as negative and recasting it as positive) as a tactic Black artists have used to handle them: instead of offering alternatives to stereotypes, you exaggerate them. That's how the Blaxploitation movies work, Hall suggests. He identifies several other artistic strategies for fighting back including offering alternative visions, and subverting form… But I'm drifting. Where's that horse?

The idea of white supremacy has forced white people to strut so much, it's absurd. I want to take this strut metaphor and ride some "white man is the devil" satire in the Malcolm X manner here. Indulge me. Strutting, chiropractors say, takes a toll on your back. All these white people wrapped up in the fantasy of white supremacy and strutting around, they need lower back massages. This is why GP surgeries are overflowing on lower back day. The *white people* (read that phrase and the rest of this paragraph in your best Malcolm X voice) have all got lower back pain, from carrying that imaginary white man's burden. The GPs can't cope. Especially now as all the migrants who used to work for the NHS have quit. Gone back home to a less hostile environment. Pity the white nightmare the racist white people fall into. They end up at a High Street acupuncture clinic in an upstairs room having needles stuck in them by what appears to them as a Chinese devil with firm hands and a hungry card reader. And in this nightmare of stereotypes that they've conjured by their own delusions, they wonder, where are all the normal acupuncture people, you know, the white ones – why is it always immigrants pummelling me and sticking needles in my back? As fast as the acupuncturist kneads those lower back muscles loose, they tense up again. No number of needles helps. The acupuncturist gets them off the bench. Try walking normally, the acupuncturist says, instead of strutting. Like me. Normal. Watch. The white client cusses and storms off. They wake from their nightmare and… promptly start strutting again!

I hope that last paragraph made you laugh. P.S. I do love how you often answer my letters and texts with links to music. I'm halfway through this letter, and I'm already wondering what music you might send me by way of response. But I'm drifting again.

We've had many laughs working out how to deal with that white strut. We've both loved intoning, in our best Malcolm X voices, "The white man is the devil!" and in this way drawing the sting, reducing the chafe of that friction, dodging the spit that white people aim at us. Because of course, we've never subscribed to the view that white people actually *are* devils, fun and cathartic though that idea is. Yet, we both walk knowing the historical reality that, as James Baldwin put it sixty years ago, most Black people "cannot risk assuming the humanity of white people is more real to them than their colour. And this leads, imperceptibly but inevitably, to a state of mind in which, having long ago learned to expect the worst, one finds it very easy to believe the worst." Yes, Naomi, we both have good white friends – friends who we know would have our backs in a fight to the death. But is it not also true that we are still wary, aware of persisting inequalities and the unfairness that generates them?

This letter has proceeded as a little dance of memory and politics, with mostly two steps forwards, one step back, a kind of shuffle of recall and reason, the general drift of which is onwards and upwards. I've spent much of the time on that one wing which looks back into my time and the time before of James Baldwin. Let me float over now to the side of youth and the future.

The Black Lives Matter movement caught me by surprise. I enjoyed marching with the young generation who organised it. It helped that Black Lives Matter blew up in the middle of lockdown. That timing added a delicious, libertarian *frisson* to the protest: defiance of the lockdown rules which everyone was so fed up with, and a perfect excuse to wear face masks so hindering the police evidence-gathering crews busy filming us for their Big Brother databases. The sun burst out, adding extra, golden-hour zest: we were being lit beautifully by God, as if the Black God up there approved our protest and was shining beneficence upon us. So too, the occasion was one of the few, truly autonomous Black protests I'd been on. It was youth-led and Instagram organised: the veteran, well-meaning, white radicals (among whom I have many dear friends) who usually take over Black political marches with their ready-to-go placards and solid Marxist slogans – were replaced during the Black Lives Matter marches by fresh-eyed youths from the local universities and streets who came with all their bright clothing, home-made campaign signs, chants both funny and serious, and earnest, heartfelt speeches. This was the realest march in decades – change was happening, and I marvelled at it: to be in lockstep with the youth of #BlackLivesMatter was briefly, to become young once more. And on that day, for the duration of that golden hour, I was young, Naomi, and shared youth's birthright of zeal and hope!

Your generation has a zeal for change and is using their energy to press for it. Everywhere, white supremacy as a concept is crumbling under that pressure. Statues are falling, university courses are being decolonised, suppressed narratives about colonialism's depredations are being set free. Lies are being thrown into the fire of truth. That is your generation's work. There will be hard times ahead. People fear change. Especially when it involves loss of power and privilege. James Baldwin imagines white people's fears: "Try to imagine how you would feel if you woke up one morning to find the sun shining and all the stars aflame..." Yet, globally, that change towards a more just and equal society is coming. Whether white people can see it or not. Whether they want it or not. It will come. The burning desire for a more just and equal society is too strong to be resisted. Such change may be beyond our current horizon. But always, the world holds more than what the eyes can see. Be assured, there is hope: the fires of tomorrow are burning.

May all your horses gallop to victory.

Godspeed.

Papa xx

James Baldwin Weeps with the Weight of Tiredness

Roy McFarlane

"I never have been in despair about the world. I've
been enraged by it. I don't think I'm in despair. I
can't afford despair. I can't tell my nephew, my niece.
You can't tell the children there's no hope."

– James Baldwin[1]

Nobody knows the trouble I've seen
Nobody knows my sorrow[2]

In the chamber of a gun, they let loose a projectile

that found its way in the chamber of Medgar Evers' heart

who spoke of humanity in the chambers of horrors of
America

and you couldn't cry, you couldn't say anything, except.

Medgar. Gone.

Nobody knows the trouble I've seen
Nobody knows but Jesus

In a restaurant in London, instead of a menu

the headwaiter informs you of a call waiting for you. Your
sister rises,

---

1 James Baldwin, interviewed by Mavis Nicholson, 12 February, 1987.
2 'Nobody Knows the Trouble I've Seen' is an African American spiritual
song that originated during the period of slavery, published 1867.

119

your sister returns as if she had been at the foot of the cross. She continues,

with formalities breaking bread, drinking wine but she can't bear it no more.

"Well, I've got to tell you because the press is on its way over here.

They just killed Malcolm."

Sometimes I'm up
Sometimes I'm down

In black & white on Pathé News they ask you about Malcolm.

You reiterate forcefully that "Malcolm was another negro man,

yet one more negro man has been murdered" – rewind the reel to the beginning,

if you watched closely, you would see a forlorn, folded body, drained and drawn,

wondering who's next.

Sometimes I'm almost to the ground
Oh, yes, Lord

In Palm Springs by a swimming pool, sitting with Billy Dee Williams,

Aretha Franklin's sweet voice flows from the radio

"a little respect (just a little bit), I get tired (just a little bit)."

James Baldwin is tired with Columbia Pictures,

after being hired to write the screenplay of Malcolm X,

James Baldwin Weeps with the Weight of Tiredness

they want to shoot him down again; re-write after re-write as if the 30 shots

that laid our brother down wasn't enough. Billy Dee's tired, always tired

of losing out to Sidney Poitier, now it looks like he might lose out

to a darkened Charlton Heston playing the role of Malcolm X.

James is tired when the phone rings, he picks up,

"Martin just been shot. He's not dead yet, but it's a head wound so…"

James dropped the phone and wept.

James Baldwin in Neuilly, France, 1970. Photo: Artstor

What's Love Got to Do with It?

Ronnie McGrath

When Jimmy Baldwin launched what I call his love revolution, held out his hand, and said to the world, "Will you be my brother, will you be my sister?", like Martin Luther King Jr, Angela Davis, and Malcolm X, he became a very dangerous human being within a system that promotes disunity. As Jimmy once said, "Love has never been a popular movement." We underestimate the power of love because today it is so easy to say those words without commitment.

"I love you" – there, I said it but what does it *really* mean? Jimmy was unrelenting in his commitment to love and did not compromise his love of humanity for anyone. Today, everybody appears to love Jimmy until they get slapped in the face by his unceasing demand to practise what the scholar and activist Dr Cornel West calls, "a radical self-critique."

For Jimmy, that beautiful, wise, saintly, Black, gay man whose eyes run deeper than rivers, it is not enough to love the familiar, to love the already known which is often safe and demands no rigour or compromise. The kind of love Jimmy talked about demands a revolution of the mind in art and life, if the two can be separated. I am all about that kind of love so when I first came across Jimmy Baldwin's work, as a Black, British, working class man on a path of self-discovery, I became an immediate disciple of his – few can resist his wisdom and charm.

Jimmy not only made me see just how fiercely intelligent

a people I came from, but he also allowed me to see the profound beauty of being Black, and how to walk with my head held high in an often-hostile white world that demanded, without any conceivable right at all, my obedience in the face of that power and privilege. I am frequently disappointed by some otherwise well-meaning Black people who see the world, particularly race, sexuality, and gender through the simplicity of a binary lens (Black/white, straight/gay) and do not account for the fact that being Black is not a singular issue. Simply put, some people are mixed race, bisexual, transgender, lesbian or queer.

However, I do understand that our trauma is real and not all of us have even begun to heal from the wounds that racism, chattel slavery, colonialism, miseducation, patriarchy, and incarceration have placed on us. The impact of such trauma passed down through generations is incalculable and it often manifests in a deep self-hatred and a profound inferiority complex. It's no wonder then that some people have turned their backs on the nuances that tangle our fate – that thorny and conflicted space where real life takes place. As Baldwin believed, it is our differences that make us the same. Baldwin held each human being to account. He was, after all, "God's witness," or as the poet Amiri Baraka said of Baldwin in his 1987 eulogy, "Jimmy was God's black revolutionary mouth." Baldwin believed that we could become much more than we are and wanted us to reach what he called, "the new Jerusalem."

Black Britons make up a small minority on these British Isles, which was once a powerful nation with an empire that controlled a quarter of the earth's surface but has yet to accept its diminishing status on the world stage. The nature of our social arrangement has meant living in large urban areas close to our white neighbours who seem to love, among many other things, our food, our music, our art and, dare I say it, our very bodies.

What's Love Got to Do with It?

This deep attraction, underpinned by both fear and desire, can sometimes manifest itself in the brutal slaying of that very Black body that the aggressor secretly adores. Furthermore, that attraction may not be straightforward because the Black body is often eroticised through the lens of exoticism. Yet, it is a testament to the human spirit, that people of different races can come together and fall in love. They often fall in love, in spite of accusations from both sides of selling out, of having mixed-race children who are supposedly 'confused' about their identity, or about their affiliations to one group of people or another. As someone who is married to a white woman, Baldwin's steadfast commitment to dismantling the myth of race, in the way he lived his life as an openly gay man who dated 'outside' his own race allowed me to do the same. The power of his insightful body of writing, his activism, and above all else his honesty and intense love of humanity, allowed me to understand the complexity of my own experience.

On a personal level, being the father of three mixed-race children (two girls who are now women, and a boy who is now a young man), has enriched both mine and my family's understanding of race in this country in nuanced ways. For example, even though my children and I share the same sense of general oppression, their particular experience of coming from a mixed-heritage background is different from my experience of growing up Black in Britain. Unlike their undeniable sense of belonging to this country – both their parents were born here – a huge part of my teenage years were spent responding, in outwardly cultural expressions of Blackness, such as donning an Afro, a dashiki, or dreads, to counter the claim that Britain was a 'white' country. The media and the 1970s school system expressed this both openly and in more subtle ways. Fuelled by a deep sense of Black pride, my friends and I steeped our identity in music and culture from Africa and Jamaica.

Baldwin taught me that Blackness was an ever-changing

same, that ultimately race was a myth, a construct, and a political category that stands between the individual and the potential blossoming of our full humanity. As Baldwin said in Karen Thorsen's 1987 documentary about his life *The Price of the Ticket,* "I am only black as long as you think you are white."

Among many other writers such as Richard Wright, Chester Himes, Caryl Phillips, and Clarence Major, Baldwin brought my attention to the fact that no matter how inconsequential I was made to feel by a society and a school system that worked against my development, the inadvertent benefit of that unfortunate experience is the insightful perspective that it granted. In other words, I was blessed with what the African American scholar, Dr W.E.B. Du Bois termed a "double consciousness"; his theory, which has negative connotations, I see as a dual self-perception that allowed me to both understand as well as embrace my being Black and British. As I alluded to earlier, today such an identity is celebrated, but in 1970s Britain, to be both Black and British was outside of the language and culture of the time.

Baldwin's unwavering love of humanity was the blueprint that allowed me to dismantle the mental slavery in which I was imprisoned. This shackle around my brain was perpetuated through a largely dysfunctional 1970s school system that used a policy known as ESN (Educationally Subnormal) to funnel otherwise bright and capable Black girls and boys into sink schools throughout London. My Black working class friends and I were taught, sometimes explicitly but often in a tacit way, to hate the 'other' which of course was ourselves. Our white working class brothers and sisters were also duped by the system but the fact of their whiteness ensured that the pole of opportunity was not as greasy. In short, I grew up in a country that tried to deny my existence and from an early age, it put me through a pernicious form of socialisation that despised the notion of difference in every form.

What's Love Got to Do with It?

However, Baldwin showed me that I could use writing as a vehicle to tell my story of growing up Black in Britain. Until my awareness of Baldwin the man, the idea that someone like me could become a writer and poet was an audacious and possibly foolish act – how would I earn enough to eat? Things were hard enough just trying to be a regular working guy on 'Maggie's farm.' After all, I had long turned my back on what I believed was a racist British education system and sought solace in the act of regular truanting. The system was doing to my friends and me what it had always intended to do and we had reverted to type. Thank God for those conscious brothers on the street, most of them Rastafarians, who steered us away from crime and planted the seeds of consciousness in our confused minds so that we could embrace our Blackness with pride. However, as grateful and blessed as I was to receive their wisdom and Afrocentric vision, it fell short of what I needed to navigate my way through a world that was Black, white, transgender, and queer.

At the time I was what was known as a 'soul boy,' and I grew up in the bosom of club culture which, in many ways, was a camp world where anything goes in terms of interracial dating and open expressions of people's sexuality – yes, we were a strange bag of night people. Although far from perfect, among other things, it was a world where one could work one's way up the hierarchy of competitive dancing and gain status in one's community by being known as a 'serious cat.' An aspect of this underground Black British club culture is captured in Isaac Julien's second feature film, *Young Soul Rebels,* as well as authentic footage which exists on YouTube titled: 'Clubbers doing the British Hustle 1978' and 'Jazz Funk Dance Music.' Venues like The WAG Club in Wardour Street, London, and The Lacey Lady, in Seven Kings, Essex, gave birth to icons and musical groups such as Sade, Mica Paris, Soul II Soul, George Michael, Loose Ends, and Linx. Britain was a country which, whether we were born here or not, flattened our differences by referring to us either as West Indians or often, the N-word. Even more disturbing was how seeds of division were sewn by the system between those who were Black British, Caribbean, and those who came directly from the continent of Africa. As someone who grew up with a Sierra Leonean stepfather and a Jamaican mother, bearing the brunt of such prejudices was a painful lived experience. Today, Black people are rightfully claiming their African heritage with a new pride.

Therefore, what I call Baldwin's love revolution was no ordinary love and not easy to enact. He demanded of us the very best that we could become. This fiercely intelligent Black gay man refused to live his life in the shadows of hypocrisy. Whether you were Black, white, gay, or indifferent, Baldwin would not let you off the hook for hating others. However, the path to forgiveness was always clear because Baldwin believed that we could always be much better than we were. He despised hatred in all its despicable forms. As his friend, Turkish writer Yashar Kamal said of the profound nature of Baldwin's work in Karen Thorsen's *The Price of the Ticket*, "Jimmy drowns you in darkness, and blinds you with light."

I am blessed to have come across the work of this great and fiercely intelligent man. I owe a lot to Baldwin for inspiring *a lickle rude and picky-headed bwoy* to have the courage to become a poet and writer, one who draws sustenance from the rich contradictions of the world we live in today, and from the wellspring of a profound 'Black' kind of love that has everything to do with being truly human.

Revisiting James Baldwin

Michael McMillan

Rereading James Baldwin's autobiographical essays, *Notes of a Native Son* (1955) and *The Fire Next Time* (1963), took me back to the time and place I first read them. I was a teenager, and it was Hackney, 1970s. It was in our living room, where my family did most of our living together, eating, watching TV, playing games, and chatting. My mother "… an extremely proud and handsome woman, with Africa, Europe, and [South East Asia] blended in her face," was usually cooking in the kitchen next to the living room, and she, sensing that I was in there, would call out, "Mikey wey yuh doing in dey?", and I would reply, "No'ting, Mummy," not wanting to tell her that I was reading, instead of the cleaning chores we were expected to do.

Being the eldest is a privilege, but also a burden (as Baldwin knew) and sometimes a curse. The eldest of four children, all British-born, of post-war Caribbean parents, the so-called Windrush generation, and I struggled, like Baldwin, to assert my identity, not simply with my father, but my mother also: I refused to see myself as 'coloured' as they expected of me, but rather as Black. Being the eldest is a double-edged sword; there is the privilege of seniority, on one level, and then the burden of responsibility, looking after eight younger siblings as Baldwin did, and setting an example for others to follow, and the curse of gendered expectation; pressures that younger siblings never quite understand. The eldest also sees things that those who follow don't. As a trial run, my parents probably felt that my rebellion was a failure on their part, because I was to them what Stuart Hall called the "trouble generation" in a "… moment of Pan-African consciousness," Black Power,

Rastafarianism, Black feminism. They were fearful for me, as Baldwin writes in *Notes of a Native Son*, with "The fear that I heard in my father's voice [...] a fear that the child, in challenging the white world's assumptions was putting himself in the path of destruction." My younger siblings observed and learnt from my rebellion, and my parents, wiser from experience, were smarter when they became teenagers.

Black young people were fed up with poor schooling, police brutality, SUS laws (Stop and Search), not being the right person for the job, being told to go back to our country, and racist attacks. So, at the first Notting Hill Carnival I attended, in the hot summer of 1976, there was a riot. The newspaper headlines read 'Blacks on the Rampage' in large bold letters. My parents went in to work the next day with shame and despair, feeling that the rioters were ungrateful for what their parents had struggled to give them. They felt the younger generation should turn the other cheek like they did, but instead we didn't want to work, and walked the streets like criminals, just as the newspapers portrayed us. As Martin Luther King Jr once said, "riots are the language of the unheard", the riots at the Notting Hill Carnival in 1976, marked what Hall called the "becoming" of unheard Black British young people expressing their identity. It was a search for an identity that I also shared with Tayo with Nigerian parents, Jiten with Indian parents, Kemal with Turkish parents, Chris with Greek Cypriot parents, my school peers born in Britain, who also experienced being othered in British society, and who felt alienated from socially compliant post-war migrant parents.

In Baldwin's 'Letter to My Nephew...' in *The Fire Next Time,* he writes, "For this is your home, my friend, do not be driven from it...". I felt as if he were talking to me personally with avuncular advice about how to survive and transcend being denied my birthright. And in a crazy fantasy, I wanted my parents, aunties and uncles to tell me, just as Baldwin tells his nephew, "We have not stopped trembling yet, but if we had not loved each other none of us would have survived. And now you must survive because we love you, and for the sake of your children and your children's children."

I went to Daneford Secondary Boys School, Bethnal Green, and mentioning their alumni included the Kray Twins, added a bit of street cred'. But, during my time there, some teachers and pupils followed the National Front, whose newspapers were sold at the Sunday market in Brick Lane nearby, and 'paki bashing' was how some white boys passed their lunchtime. Bangladeshi boys were let home early so they wouldn't get stabbed, and in response to police indifference towards racist attacks, they formed vigilantes for self-defence. The school also attracted left-wing teachers with Trotskyite, anarchist and socialist tendencies, and amongst them was my English teacher, Norman Goodman, who like Baldwin's teacher, Bill Miller, took me and other boys to the theatre. Mr Goodman sensed that I was becoming politicised and opened his locked classroom wooden cupboard to his collection of literature that was not on the curriculum. This is where I found Baldwin's works, along with George Jackson's *Soledad Brother*, Eldridge Cleaver's *Soul on Ice*, George Orwell's *1984* and *Animal Farm*.

I edited and wrote for a short-lived school magazine, and Mr Goodman encouraged me to enter an essay competition advertised in *The West Indian World*, with the prize to attend *FESTAC 77* (The 2nd World Festival of Black Arts and Culture) in Lagos and Kaduna, Nigeria, 1977. More an exercise in putting down in words what I wanted to say, than winning, I sent in a righteous essay entitled 'Power to the Black Youth'. To my shock, I won, and at fifteen, having never had a passport, never been on a plane, never been to Africa, much less Nigeria, I attended *FESTAC 77* for three weeks. At this impressionable age, it was a transformative experience, especially witnessing as an informal 'runner', the production process for Michael Abbensetts' play, *Sweet Talk*, which was performed in the National Theatre. I wanted the creative power that Abbensetts seemed to possess, and inspired by Shelagh Delaney's play, *A Taste of Honey,* that we were studying at school, I wrote my first play, *The School Leaver*, and sent it to the Royal Court Theatre's Young Writers Festival. It was selected and produced in 1978.

Recalling Baldwin's arduous relationship with his stepfather as described in *Notes of a Native Son* reminded me of my relationship with my father. I loved him and I knew he loved us, working every hour God sent to provide for his family, but it nearly drove him mad, and I despised him for taking that anger out on my mother. I wrote about what I knew in *The School Leaver*, but after my parents saw its premiere with me at the Royal Court Theatre, there was silence in the black cab we took from Sloane Square to our home in Hackney. I knew they were proud of me, but I also knew they were confused about the story their son had created. With the subsequent publicity and attention I received, my parents assumed that my achievement was a pathway to getting a 'proper' job. But growing up in a working class family like Baldwin, my aspiration to become a writer caused consternation, though unlike him, it was my mother who felt that I had lost my way.

The poet, Nikki Giovanni, interviewed Baldwin in a famous 1971 televised conversation. Afro-haired Nikki was twenty-eight, and Baldwin was nearly fifty. As writer and performer, Vanessa Kisuule says in her essay, 'Reviving the Ambivalence' for WritersMosaic's guest edition, *Going to meet James Baldwin*, "Baldwin smiles at her like a fond uncle at his precocious niece." And an avuncular Baldwin tries to make Giovanni understand the struggles of being a Black man in America, though she pushes back, arguing that Black women are also unloved. For me, Giovanni, alongside Angela Davis, Michele Faith Wallace, Audre Lorde, Alice Walker, bell hooks to mention a few, represent Black feminist writing and thinking that has impacted my formation. If I had met Baldwin in my twenties, like Giovanni, I also would adore him as a writer, whose shoulders I stand on, but I would also challenge him on the question of gender, and that regardless of the trials and tribulations life throws at us, we still make choices about what we do about that lived experience.

I'm sure Giovanni would agree that it is respectability through the lens of patriarchy within the church that forces Sister Margaret Alexander to choose between her career as a pastor, and commitment as a mother and spouse, to her family in the climax of Baldwin's play *The Amen Corner* (1968). Of the different performances of the play I have seen over the years, it was Marianne Jean Baptiste, as Sister Margaret in the National Theatre's 2013 production, who laid bare this dilemma with a fierce intelligence when she proclaimed, "Who'd ever want to love a man and raise a child!" With the man she didn't marry dying in her home, and their son leaving the church, she is judged for choosing the 'Holy Ghost' over her family, and about to lose her ministry.

The dying man is Luke, who Sister Margaret left after she lost their child giving birth. Luke's son, David wants to be a musician like his father, and in a tender scene, father and son express their love for each other in spite of their anguish and regret. In a touching moment, acknowledging his son's manhood, Luke says to David, "Didn't know you was smoking already. Let's have a cigarette." They go on to have a painful, but liberating conversation, one that Baldwin might have wished he had with his father, and one which I was lucky to have with my father in his later years after I became a father, and realised that in some ways, I was like him. For me, it was a moment superbly described by Baldwin in *The Fire Next Time* with the words, "Love takes off the masks that we fear we cannot live without and know we cannot live within."

Baldwin's stepfather was a preacher, and he became one at

fourteen, where giving weekly sermons over four years became "… my sustenance, my meat and drink." It is the culture of the Black church that Baldwin brings into being in his first novel, *Go Tell It on the Mountain* (1953), and likewise in *The Amen Corner*, where church members, as Sister Margaret declares, live and judge each other by scriptural doctrine, "They don't drink, they don't smoke, they don't play cards, they don't covet their neighbour's husband or their neighbour's wife – well amen!"

But as Baldwin confesses in 'Down at the Cross: Letter from a Region in My Mind' in *Notes of a Native Son*, "Some went on wine or whiskey or the needle, and are still on it. And others, like me, fled into the church." It was adolescent impulses as a teenage young man that meant church became a hiding place, just as it was for Sister Margaret, who "… is in the church because her society has left her no other place to go." But eventually facing himself, Baldwin becomes disenchanted with the church as a place of "Blindness, Loneliness, and Terror" rather than "Faith, Hope, and Charity." My parents weren't as fundamentalist as Baldwin's parents, but they did expect my siblings and I to attend church, as well as Sunday school, more out of a sense of moral responsibility than religious zeal. Like Baldwin, becoming a teenager was a transformative moment for me, and my political formation like many Black youth at the time, was informed by reggae music, with lyrics such as those in Bob Marley's 'Crazy Baldhead' (1976):

> "Build your penitentiary
> we build your schools
> brainwash education
> to make us the fools
> hate is your reward for our love
> telling us of your God above."

On a WritersMosaic panel at the British Library on 27th March 2024 celebrating James Baldwin's centenary, the novelist and critic, Mendez, said that Baldwin wrote how he spoke, with the cadence of a preacher. Mendez has a point; it is Baldwin's lyrical rhythmic eloquence in his legendary performance in the 1965 Cambridge Union debate with William F. Buckley, for instance, that we read in the erudite measured poise of his prose.

Raoul Peck's documentary, *I Am Not Your Negro* (2016) draws on Baldwin's unfinished memoir, *Remember This House*, in which he tells his story of America through the lives of three of his murdered friends: Medgar Evers, Malcolm X and Martin Luther King Jr. Samuel L. Jackson provides a voiceover narration of Baldwin's words, which is interspersed with archive footage of television interviews with Baldwin and him talking in Horace Ové's 1968 documentary, *Baldwin Nigger*, and the events surrounding the assassinations of Medgar, Malcolm and Martin.

In response to Martin's murder in 1968, African Americans had had enough, and took to the streets across America, and footage here blends in an uncanny, terrifying but familiar way with 2014 protests and uprisings in Ferguson, Missouri, over the police killing of Michael Brown. And in giving voice to what became the Black Lives Matter movement, Peck's film foretells how Black communities across the diaspora would respond to another police killing of a Black man – George Floyd, in 2020. Baldwin's words that, "History is not in the past, but in the present, because we carry our histories with us," have a poignant prescience that haunt me, because when thinking about George's killing, I remember David Oluwale, Colin Roach, Christopher Alder, just a few Black men in the UK, who since 1969, have been the fatal victims of police violence on the street or in custody. Yet we notice that the populist mainstream discourse deploys tremendous labour to forget the past, or at least to portray a happy smiling-face version of history, as if the past has no relevance to our dark present.

And in trying to accept my own past, and learning how to use it, Baldwin's line at the end of *Notes of a Native Son* comes to mind: "I want to be an honest man and a good writer." Reflecting upon my younger self through the lens of age with Baldwin at my side, I know that the constant has been trying to be true to oneself with integrity as I strive to be an honest man and a good writer.

Bibliography
Stuart Hall 'The "West Indian" Front Room', *The Front Room: Diaspora Migrant Aesthetics in the Home,* ed. Michael McMillan, London: Lund Humphries, 2023, p24

Six Degrees of James Baldwin

Tony Medina

On a humble, I joined the military to make money for college. By then, I knew I wanted to be a writer but was trying to figure out how to get there beyond an obsessive diet of reading books.

When I got out of the army, after a three-year stint, the only college on my mind was Baruch College (CUNY), ten blocks away from my high school, Norman Thomas. I got out of the army on the heels of Baldwin's funeral, which I watched on Gil Noble's show *Like It Is,* that focused on issues pertaining to Black and Brown communities.

At Baruch, I majored in English because I loved to read and write. As luck would have it, my first professor was Addison Gayle Jr who kept name-dropping his famous literary friends – and he was good friends with James Baldwin. Every now and then, Dr Gayle would pivot and go off on tangents about his life and experiences – they were some of the best parts of the class, because he regaled us with the rich exploits of the life of the writer. He started talking about "Jimmy" – as in Baldwin – as in my favourite writer, and how generous he was. Gayle would tell us how James Baldwin would invite him to crash at his famous crib in the South of France, whenever he was in town. Baldwin moved to Paris when he was nineteen. He was broke and struggling to make it as a writer. Writers like Richard Wright, and other friends, helped him immensely. Baldwin's generosity most likely sprang from this pay-it-forward attitude because of how others had helped him.

I heard more stories from Dr Eleanor Taylor (former chair of the Department of English at Howard University), who brought me to Howard to teach Creative Writing. Eleanor would tell me how she, Toni Morrison, and Toni Cade Bambara would spend weeks at James Baldwin's crib in the South of France editing Bambara's latest manuscript, or working on their own projects, writing, and drinking, and having much-needed fabulous powerhouse sister-girl time away from the powder keg of America.

*

A decade has passed since I was on stage beside Amiri Baraka's open casket, speaking at his funeral on January 18th, 2014, held in the Sarah Vaughan Concert Hall in Newark. I had first encountered Amiri Baraka in the late 1980s, at his basement poetry café, Kimako's Blues People, named after his sister who was murdered by a homeless man whom she had befriended and taken in. I recall Martín Espada, who was a featured poet that night (and who was being celebrated for receiving a Guggenheim Fellowship), telling me after my first public reading, "Amiri really likes your stuff." I finally spoke with Amiri, following that evening's readings and jazz performance. He noticed my copy of *The Fire Next Time*, and said of Baldwin, "That was a deep brother." He also told me how Baldwin had visited him in Newark at the height of the Black Arts Movement, and how on a tour of the neighbourhood, kids had bumrushed the famous Black writer. It was that image I took back with me to my tiny apartment in The Bronx. That, and my sighting of a signed copy of a framed Langston Hughes' poem in Amiri's vestibule which read: "To that boy LeRoi."

I recall other memories with Amiri at a Spoken Word Jam for Mumia Abu-Jamal at the Apollo Theatre soundstage in 1999, celebrating the anthology *In Defense of Mumia* which I co-edited with Sam Anderson, a founding New York Black Panther. Amiri introduced me to Max Roach there. Another time, at one of the CUNY schools, I got to hang out with Amiri and Dr Gayle in the green room right before a Black literature panel.

Six Degrees of James Baldwin

When I was a college student and a young, hungry poet wanting to make my bones as a writer, I deliberately sought out my elders, first by reading them and then by meeting them. Writers don't usually seek anyone out to mentor – they get jacked by the mentee who bumrushes the professor after class, as I did with Dr Gayle. I did the same with others like Miguel Algarín, Sam Anderson and Amiri Baraka, following them around like a puppy dog, asking questions, questions, questions, and above all, learning to be quiet and listen. The art of writing is listening. I've played the role of mentor myself for many but it seems that when students have access to a writer, they don't often take advantage of that opportunity, they don't ask questions and never learn anything about the writer-professor beyond the classroom.

*

Dr Gayle sadly died of a double stroke while I was still a student at Baruch College. I had ploughed through Gayle's prodigious output of memoir and criticism from Baruch College's library stacks in my first semester. He was my first literary mentor. When I attended his funeral, I met one of my literary heroes, Claude Brown, whose book, *Manchild in the Promised Land,* had influenced me. I also met Haki R. Madhubuti (born as Don L. Lee) at the funeral through my literature professor, Saundra Towns. She introduced us by saying, "Haki, this is Tony Medina – he's a great poet, you should publish him!" Haki, who was one of my favourite poets, would later become one of my publishers.

*

I recall an interview with Suzan-Lori Parks (I read with her at the New School back in the early 1990s), in which she talked of her professor, James Baldwin, at Amherst and how the real class did not begin until they all migrated from the classroom to a local bar, after class. It was then that Baldwin told Parks that she was not a novelist but a playwright – and that totally changed her life. Although she also went on to publish a novel, her major work is in the theatre where she has become a highly successful prize-winning playwright.

It was James Baldwin who taught me how to write! Like a musician who plays by ear, I learned to write through reading. Growing up, I had no role models for reading (I can hear echoes of Lucille Clifton's poem 'won't you celebrate with me' where she says, "I had no model!") nor was I surrounded by books in my household. The only person I ever saw reading was my paternal grandmother who would read her Bible daily and the occasional cheap, paperback novel. Other than that, television was my literature (or better yet, my way of accessing stories beyond the storytelling embedded in household gossip).

It took an F-grade on a book report that I neglected to do to set me on the road to reading, and eventually writing, when I was in the 9th grade. After Mr De Los Reyes handed out another copy of the booklist he gave us at the beginning of the school year, and not wanting to disappoint my grandmother (who raised me), or him, I went to the library to look for a book to write about. The book that attracted my attention was *Flowers for Algernon* by Daniel Keyes. I was intrigued by the title because I didn't know what the hell an Algernon was.

The Throg's Neck Library, located outside Throg's Neck Housing projects along the Cross Bronx Expressway, was a place I usually ducked into with my friends to escape the cold, or in the summer, to escape the heat and quench our thirst with the cold water from the electric fountain. The librarian taught me how to use the card catalogue system to find the book I wished to borrow. When I found it, I was delighted that the book was there, and not the size of *Moby Dick* or the telephone book. It was a little over two hundred pages, something I felt confident I could handle, even though I had never really read an entire book on my own.

When I got home that evening, I started reading the novel

and was so elated, I couldn't put it down until that Sunday night, when I started to write the book report. I received an A+ for the first time, and announced to my family that I was going to be a writer. One aunt bought me a typewriter, another bought me a desk, and I began saving my allowance (usually reserved for candy or chips) to buy paperback books. Reading became my obsession. My other obsession was haunting bookstores. If I felt melancholy, depressed, or lonely, I'd find myself in a bookstore. If I liked a book by a writer, say John Steinbeck, I'd read everything Steinbeck wrote and everything written about Steinbeck. Then I'd read the blurbs other authors wrote endorsing the book, then I'd search out their books, too. This is still my reading process today.

While in high school I worked part-time as a messenger as part of my marketing major. During deliveries, I'd dip into a bookstore in Penn Station and peruse the poetry and fiction sections. On two occasions I noticed Black and Brown faces on the covers of books and this had a profound effect on me. One was *Selected Poems of Langston Hughes* which has a photo of him at his typewriter looking over his left shoulder at the camera, with a thin black moustache and wavy hair. I felt an immediate connection with Langston; he looked like someone in my family. And when I opened the book, the poems were about people from the 'hood. It was about Harlem where my family is from, and the street scenes and the depictions of the everyday people in his poems deeply affected my psyche. I got the same jolt of electricity when I saw James Baldwin's headlight eyes staring deep into my soul from the cover of *The Fire Next Time*. In the epistolary essays to his nephew, Baldwin schools him on who he is, where he came from, and what he should expect – but not accept – being a Black man-child in an unforgiving America that eats its young. When I read, 'Fifth Avenue, Uptown', it was about the same Harlem streets that my father was born and raised in, where he was a shoeshine boy for Detroit Red (who became Malcolm X), when he slang dope for Nicky Barnes and did a seven-year bid in Sing Sing. It was the same Harlem where my father saw John Coltrane play and heard Billie Holiday sing.

But beyond the familiarity with Baldwin's subject matter concerning Harlem, his struggles with Christianity, Blackness, his sexual identity, and his growing inclination of wanting to be a writer, I learned how to write by reading and studying Baldwin's long-ass, page-length, perfectly punctuated sentences. Baldwin literally wrote like he spoke, probably from his boyhood preacher days or the sermonizing oral tradition he was raised in. Reading his essays is like being in a conversation with him. I would read his sentences a thousand times to figure out how he managed to write such long, eloquent sentences and never skip a beat with his meticulous punctuation. He goes off on tangents, then circles back to his main topic, and you never get lost in the labyrinth of his sentences. It was then that I started to read not just for pleasure but to learn how to use punctuation and grammar outside of the incomprehensible lessons that English teachers were spewing (like the grown-ups in a *Peanuts* cartoon) which seemed to go in one ear and out the other. Baldwin provided me with ocular proof, as Othello put it, to see how each punctuation mark served a particular purpose, and that if you were missing a comma or misplaced one, you could throw the entire meaning off. Baldwin taught me to be a conscious reader, as well as a conscious writer.

As I was learning to write in those critical teenage years, I was being politicized while absorbing his origin story. And because there was always a deep well of compassion amid Baldwin's passion and rages at a society that daily denied Black people's humanity, I absorbed lessons in honesty and growth from essay to essay, book to book. Baldwin also admitted to his youthful indiscretions such as publicly tearing down Black literary father figures like Richard Wright and Langston Hughes, both of whom he had ravaged in book reviews and essays, only later to regret it, after rethinking his position.

Six Degrees of James Baldwin

What I essentially learned from James Baldwin was how to fight and defend myself with words. It was this indelible influence that I gleaned as a teen that equipped and armed me with the agency to navigate and negotiate the racism I encountered and grappled with throughout my life. Language was Baldwin's way of liberating his future. And although he parted with his child preacher past and broke from the constraints of the Christian church, he never veered too far from its moral compass. He often referred to his writing as "bearing witness." I'm reminded of Baldwin's approach to this ethos, and how wherever he went in the world, he witnessed connection and the familiar.

As a young struggling writer, Baldwin frequented the Left Bank of Paris, lived in the Arab Quarter, and identified with the Algerians who were colonized by the French. He once wrote of Paris, "I lived mainly among *les misérables* – and in Paris *les misérables* are Algerian." He chronicled this in his fascinating book, *No Name in the Street*, the title of which derives from Job 18:17-18: "His remembrance shall perish from the earth, and He shall have no name in the street. He shall be driven from light into darkness and chased out of the world."

> "[My] reasons for coming to France, and the comparative freedom of my life in Paris, meant that my attitude toward France was very different from that of any Algerian. He, and his brothers, were, in fact, being murdered by my hosts. And Algeria, after all, is a part of Africa, and France, after all, is a part of Europe [...] from which, in sober truth, Africa has yet to liberate herself. The fact that I had never seen the Algerian casbah was of no more relevance before this unanswerable panorama than the fact that the Algerians had never seen Harlem. The Algerian and I were both, alike, victims of this history, and I was still a part of Africa, even though I had been carried out of it nearly four hundred years before."

Before he settled on Paris, Baldwin considered a kibbutz in the newly-established Israel as a landing place, as he was initially in favour of this state created by the brutal removal of Palestinians. Throughout his life, Baldwin, like others in the Black activist tradition, had strong ties with members of the Jewish community. He attended DeWitt Clinton High School in The Bronx with Jewish classmates like Emile Capouya, Richard Avedon, and Sol Stein with whom he worked on the school magazine, *The Magpie*, and who early on considered him a genius. It was in *The Magpie* that Baldwin interviewed one of his early literary mentors, Countee Cullen. He was even mentored at PS 139 (Frederick Douglass Junior High School) by Orrin "Bill" Miller, a leftist Jewish white woman schoolteacher from the Midwest, who took an interest in the precocious young Baldwin, though his religious conflicts undermined that profound relationship. Baldwin maintained ties with Jewish intellectuals in the activist and literary intelligentsia at home in New York and abroad during his self-imposed exile. But at the height of the Civil Rights movement and Black Power struggles of the 1960s and 1970s, and off the heels of his activist friends Medgar Evers, Dr Martin Luther King Jr, and Malcolm X, being assassinated, Baldwin's thinking on the Israeli settlement leaned towards seeing Israel as an occupying force and a satellite of American and European socio-political economic interests.

Like any honest intellectual worth his salt, Baldwin was constantly evolving and growing. He used his observations, analysis, and life story as material for his short stories, novels, plays, poetry, and essays. I'd like to think that one of my favourite novels of his, *If Beale Street Could Talk*, about a young Black artist falsely accused of raping a woman, was inspired by Baldwin's own experience at fourteen, when he was abducted by two white cops, dragged into a Harlem alley, and pummelled just for shits and giggles. Had he lived to celebrate his centenary, Baldwin, as elder statesman, would certainly be at the forefront commenting on and mentoring those of us in the Black Lives Matter movement.

Six Degrees of James Baldwin

I think about the six degrees of separation concept every time I say, "James Baldwin taught me how to write," because he was as impactful to me as he was for other writers who had known him personally. I sometimes reflect on how I became the writer I am today – how it was Baldwin's face on the cover of *The Fire Next Time* that initially captivated me. Then his words. About Harlem. And by extension – about me.

Of James Baldwin and Futures Not Seen

Bill V. Mullen

"… we live in an age in which silence is not only
criminal but suicidal."

— James Baldwin, 'An Open Letter to
My Sister Angela Davis', 1970

What would James Baldwin do? I've asked myself that question
many times as this centennial year of his birth spins backwards,
reproducing the worst of the last century. The "silence"
Baldwin warned us not to fall into screams out: about the
genocide Israel is perpetuating against Gaza as I write; about
the global rise and resurgence of far-right, white nationalist,
xenophobic, governments and movements; about the mass-
scale targeting of queer, non-binary, and trans people who
embody a crisis of the human from reactive capitalist forces
which seek to return us to a state of 'nature' under which the
planet itself shudders and quakes.

Baldwin would have been outraged by all of this, surprised
by none of it. He was less a prophet than a historical
materialist, seeing the arc of future histories written in the
granular detail of present contradictions. In 1979, thirty-one
years into Israel's occupation of Palestine, and nearly a full
decade before the First Intifada, Baldwin warned in 'Open
Letter to the Born Again' that "the state of Israel was not
created for the salvation of the Jews; it was created for the
salvation of the Western interests [...] The Palestinians have
been paying for the British colonial policy of 'divide and rule'

and for Europe's guilty Christian conscience for more than thirty years… there is absolutely – repeat: *absolutely* – no hope of establishing peace in what Europe so arrogantly calls the Middle East (how in the world would Europe know? having so dismally failed to find a passage to India) without dealing with the Palestinians."[1] Baldwin's prescient dedication to Black-Palestinian solidarity was rooted in an understanding of how anti-Blackness, Islamophobia and anti-Arab racism were forged in sites of colonial atrocity like Algeria, or Parisian jails, where he learned from North African colonial subjects, as he put it, that "as I began to discern what their history had made of them, I began to suspect, somewhat painfully, what my history had made of me."[2]

And Baldwin long ago saw the threat of what we euphemistically call in 2024 the Far Right, or Neo-Fascism, as on a continuum with centuries of Western slavery, colonialism, and capitalism. In his 1970 letter to Angela Davis cited above, Baldwin compared Davis to a Jewish woman en route to the gas chambers at Dachau, a reminder of both his longstanding abhorrence of anti-Semitism, and his foreknowledge that what Davis called the "law-enforcement-judicial-penal apparatus" could be the basis for an "incipient" American fascism. Baldwin saw American fascism creep closer, in the figure of Ronald Reagan, who as Governor of California had hastened Davis's arrest and frame-up, and as President allied himself with the most savage forms of American capitalism.

In his poem 'Staggerlee Wonders,' Baldwin compared Reagan to a Hollywood *doppelgänger*: the white vigilante John Wayne, killer of filmic Indians, purveyor of war against real and imaginary Vietnamese.[3] Indeed Baldwin, who wrote a brilliant book of film criticism, *The Devil Finds Work,* would I think have found the 2024 Oscar and BAFTA-award winning film *Oppenheimer* appalling: not a single Japanese person appears in a three-hour film about the massacre of more than two million Japanese. In 1961, after having joined the advisory board for SANE (National Committee for a Sane Nuclear Policy), Baldwin wrote that "racial hatred and the atom bomb both threaten the destruction of man as created by God."[4]

And Baldwin – border and boundary-crossing queer of colour that he was – would have shaken at the dungeon of our rabidly heteronormative 2024 world hardening every day to criminalize, or regulate, or eliminate, gender non-conformists. As Alberto Toscano has put the matter in his recent book about sexual tyrannists and "late" fascists: "Where the migrant of colour is the avatar of the Great Replacement, the eventual extinction of whiteness and its component nations, transness is the emblem and emissary of a Great Disorder, the scrambling of sexual difference and the destruction of the family [...] For them, the decline of the West *is* gender trouble [...]" [5]

In his 1985 essay 'Here Be Dragons,' Baldwin, opining on a previous generation's challenge to the sexual order of things, perceived the drive for patriarchal restoration in eerily similar terms. "Such figures as Boy George do not disturb me nearly so much as do those relentlessly hetero (sexual?) keepers of the keys and seals, those who know what the world needs in the way of order and who are ready and willing to supply that order. This rage for order can result in chaos, and in this country, chaos connects with color."[6]

The analytical life James Baldwin lived begs a second version of the question: What would James Baldwin *do*? Baldwin publicly married the role of artist to the role of public radical in his lifetime. He was never, ever, without an organization, or group or coalition, or collective, even when he was deep into writing. Baldwin's desperate desire for *communitas* was why he marched, wrote public letters, raised funds for prisoners, allied with the Panthers, challenged the FBI, signed petitions for Cuba, organized against the Kennedy White House, spoke at mass rallies from London to Oakland, sought out audiences of school children and youth, flamed queer in both public and private life. This rabble-rousing Baldwin has been partly resurrected by the Black Lives Matter movement, which has seen in Baldwin's *words* an avatar of *action*. Baldwin's description of police as "occupying" armies in Black neighborhoods took on the mantle of a 'Call to Arms' as demonstrators flooded the streets to mourn and rage for the lives of Tamir Rice, Sandra Bland, George Floyd, Laquan McDonald, and far, far too many other Black youths shot down by police. My own estimate is that Baldwin would have been at the head of every #BlackLivesMatter protest he could reach had he lived to see it. His "next" book would be about the moment of crisis he was living through with us, whatever it happened to be. As if channeling that very aspiration, so many Black writers and artists taking up #BlackLivesMatter and police violence in the past ten years have turned to Baldwin as paradigm and inspiration for their own work: Ta-Nehisi Coates, Jesmyn Ward, Teju Cole, Raoul Peck, Barry Jenkins, not to mention the thousands of social media activists and agitators, like the creator of the website 'Son of Baldwin.' [7]

And I have wondered, too, where would Baldwin position himself today in the mass struggle for LGBTQ+ rights? Despite his provocative, admiring, transformative conversations with Audre Lorde, and despite his very public pronouncements on the "prison" of heteronormativity, Baldwin in 1984, even as the AIDs epidemic soared, remained almost circumspect in conversation with Richard Goldstein about the "so-called" gay movement that was erupting across the US.[8] Baldwin's gentle defense of private sexuality and private life was beginning to sound archaic in the face of ACT UP and the rise in Queer visibility. The writer who wrote *Giovanni's Room,* so far ahead of its time as to be from another world, sometimes sounded in the 1980s like a man out of time.

Which I think he always was, and why I think the answer to

the question, "What would James Baldwin *do*?" is as contingent now as it was then. Only he would have been able to answer it with any degree of satisfaction. That is in part because I believe Baldwin always lived with one foot in a world of possibility and things "not seen" – the keywords for his 1985 book on the Atlanta child murders.[9] His persistent pessimism of the intellect, optimism of the will, as Gramsci put it, always meant that his best ideas were the *next* ideas, the ones that had not yet formed but were in formation. Baldwin lived in a space between the world as it was and the world that he wished for and imagined. "I'm optimistic about the future," he told John Hall in 1970, in what is still my favourite Baldwin quote, "but not about the future of this civilization. I'm optimistic about the civilization that will replace this one."[10]

This is not the end-time millennialism of a conspiracy theorist, but the earned, agentive vision of someone who made history as much as it made him. Baldwin was the great *doer* of the 20th century's great American writers. He was a real-life revolutionary, a Harlem-born, global north version of the Frantz Fanons and Ding Lings and Agnes Smedleys and Tillie Olsens and Jose Martis, and Ghassan Kanafanis who lived their 20th-century lives committed to a two-sided struggle in which art and political change co-constitute each other in a kind of dance of transformative possibilities.

The reason James Baldwin continues to sound like the moment we live in is because he perceived in the present both the conditions of the past and the potentialities of the future. What James Baldwin would *do* in 2024 is the same thing he did every year of his life on earth: make expressible and urgent and understandable that human beings make history not under the circumstances of their choosing but because we have no choice but to make change happen.

Notes

1. 'Open Letter to the Born Again', *The Nation*, Sept. 29, 1979.

2. 'The Price of the Ticket', in *James Baldwin Collected Essays.* Ed. Toni Morrison, New York: Library of America, 1998 p. 835.

3. James Baldwin. 'Staggerlee Wonders'. *Poetry Foundation*. https://www.poetryfoundation.org/poems/88885/staggerle-e-wonders

4. Vincent Intondi, '#blacklivesmatter and the Bomb: The Connected History of Racism, Colonialism, Freedom and Peace.' *Sojourners,* July 29, 2015. https://sojo.net/articles/blacklivesmat-ter-and-bomb

5. Alberto Toscano, *Late Fascism: Race, Capitalism, and the Politics of Crisis,* New York, Verso, 2023.

6. James Baldwin, 'Here Be Dragons' in *The Price of the Ticket: Collected Nonfiction 1948-1985*, Boston: Beacon Press, 2021, pp. 689.

7. Jesmyn Ward, Ed. Ta-Nehisi Coates, *Between the World and Me*, New York: One World, 2015;
The Fire This Time: A New Generation Speaks about Race. New York: Scribner, 2017; Teju Cole, *Known and Strange Things: Essays,* New York: Random House, 2016; Raoul Peck, Dir. *I Am Not Your Negro* (2016), Barry Jenkins, Dir. *If Beale Street Could Talk* (2018); Robert Jones, Jr, 'Son of Baldwin' https://www.sonof-baldwin.com/

8. 'Go the Way Your Blood Beats.' James Baldwin interview with Richard Goldstein, *Village Voice,* June 26, 1984. Republished in *James Baldwin: The Last Interview*, Brooklyn: Melville House, 2014, p. 7.

9. James Baldwin, *The Evidence of Things Not Seen,* New York: Holt, Rinehart, and Winston, 1985.

10. 'James Baldwin Interviewed.' First published in *Transatlantic Review*, 37-38 (Autumn–Winter 1970–71), pp. 5-14; Reprinted in *Conversations with James Baldwin,* Ed. Fred L. Standley and Louis H. Pratt, Jackson: University Press of Mississippi, 1989, p. 102.

The Fire is Now

Nducu wa Ngugi

I sit in my father's home office in my village in Kenya, surrounded by hundreds of books, papers, and binders full of articles, handwritten notes, and correspondence. I hear my mother, Nyambura wa Ngugi, calling me. She needs me to run to the store. It is a tumultuous, uncertain time for me. I have just completed the Certificate of Primary Exam, and my future, it feels, hangs in the balance. If I fail, it will be a personal defeat, and I'll have to retake the test the following year. If I do well, I am guaranteed a spot in a secondary school. In 1977, almost a year earlier, my father, Ngugi wa Thiong'o, had been detained without trial in Kamiti Maximum Security Prison. It is, I am told, for working with the peasants and workers of Kamirithu village to stage a play called *Ngaahika Ndeenda [I Will Marry When I Want]*, co-written with Ngugi wa Mirii. The play tackles class struggle, poverty, gender dynamics, cultural identity, religious influences, the conflict between modernity and tradition, etc. It is critical of the post-independence government of the time. My mother has assured me that she is still doing everything possible to bring him home. I know she will. She has that quiet resolve and determination that carries love. At eleven or twelve, I am old enough to understand the difficulties ahead, but she keeps us all moving proudly and fearlessly towards tomorrow.

She calls again. I hear her, but I am distracted. I am skimming through a book by James Baldwin, *Go Tell It on the Mountain*. I run out with the book to meet my mother and ask her if she had ever met him. She smiles and says she never met Baldwin, but they had visited Harlem, New York, and she will tell me about it when I return from the store. She and my father had travelled to the United States and stayed for a year or so in Chicago, where my father taught English and African Literature at Northwestern University.

Years later, I sit in a lecture hall at Oberlin College, Ohio, listening to Professor Calvin Hernton. His talk centres around his critical text, *Sex and Racism in America*. I am particularly interested in his life in the Black Arts Movement (BAM) in the 1960s and the parallels he draws between the BAM and the Harlem Renaissance. He mentions titles such as *Native Son* by Richard Wright and *Manchild in the Promised Land* by Claude Brown and authors and activists such as Nikki Giovanni, Angela Davis, and many other writers from that period. It is spirited writing, he says. It is urgent and steeped in the history that produced it. As his talk progresses, it swirls around the Civil Rights Movement, the AIDS epidemic, and the Rodney King riots in Los Angeles.

"James Baldwin told us about the fire next time," I hear a voice from the back of the room, "but the fire is now." There is a cheer from the primarily Black audience, many of whom share my residence at the Afrikan Heritage House (we call it "The House"). I turn, but the speaker has sat down. Professor Hernton smiles and says something about James Baldwin being a cool cat. I like the sound of that.

James Baldwin... I let the familiar name roll on my tongue as the debate on race relations, Blackness and self-love, the prison industrial complex, and the white power structure in America rages on. My mind wanders back to the quiet in my parents' home office, where I first met the words of Black writers of the Harlem Renaissance and BAM in books and magazines. Later that evening, I find a corner in the college library. I immerse myself in learning more about this "cool cat" James Baldwin.

Apart from what I call a transcendental vision of Black love, compassionate resistance, and belonging, there is something resolutely fiery in James Baldwin's writing. It is urgent yet beguiling, fierce yet unflustered, powerful without pretension, and peacefully present without disregarding a violent past. It is writing that is alive. It has foresight. It is prophetic. It speaks of the exigency of the now. It articulates the need to stand firm in the beauty of our skin. It demands confrontation with an America that is dishonest about its past and willfully ignorant of its present condition. I feel the passion and commitment and the compelling need to act. And I read on.

Baldwin lays bare the trajectory of American life in *The Fire Next Time* (a non-fiction book containing two essays). In the first one, 'My Dungeon Shook,' an open letter to his nephew, James, he says:

"[…] You are tough, dark, vulnerable, moody – with
a very definite tendency to sound truculent because
you don't want anyone to think you are soft."

I feel something inside me move. These words carry a weight that anchors and centres me and then holds a mirror in which I see myself. I hear his soft but clear voice, asking me to believe in myself and not the image someone has ascribed to my existence.

The words take me back to Kenya. I am a young man in secondary school. I have huge ambitions. However, the assurance of democratic spaces for creative expression and self-actualization that come with independence is being snuffed out. The retrogressive regimes of President Kenyatta and then the dictator Daniel arap Moi have silenced dissent, and those who dare speak out are either exiled or locked in state prisons on trumped-up charges.

My father is forced into exile after learning of plans to assassinate him. My mother is once again the pillar that holds us together. Their telephone calls deliver whispered greetings and encouragement for us, the children, who move quickly between sorrow and laughter. It is this love that keeps us connected and focused. We read, tell stories, sing, and play. Life must go on even amid uncertainty. And then the break-ins to our home begin. My mother suffers a gushing wound to her forehead inflicted by armed robbers who have broken in and ransacked our house at night. Neighbours and friends have also turned away; some cross the street to avoid a meeting. Someone might be watching, they say. Fear causes paralysis, and self-preservation becomes blinding, so the visitors who came during the good times have dried up. We are left alone to perish.

"We cannot allow them to tear us apart," our mother tells us. Her voice is full of affection, and it warms my heart. This is a profound kind of love. I bask in it.

James Baldwin speaks the same kind of love and wisdom. He urges his nephew not to wallow in bitterness at the hurt he must endure, the humiliating trauma that led his grandfather to holiness and death. Baldwin writes:

> "I know what the world has done to my brother and how narrowly he has survived it. And I know, which is much worse, and this is the crime of which I accuse my country and my countrymen, and for which neither I nor time nor history will ever forgive them, for that they have destroyed and are destroying hundreds of thousands of lives and do not know it and do not want to know it. One can be, and indeed, one must strive to become, tough and philosophical concerning destruction and death, for this is what most of mankind has been best at since we have heard of man. (But, remember: most of mankind is not all of mankind.) But it is not permissible that the authors of devastation should also be innocent. It is the innocence which constitutes a crime."

Baldwin challenges me to understand this world and my participation in it. I appreciate his passion, quest for acceptance, and even love for those who have done so much harm, for they do not know what they are doing. They are lost, "trapped in a history that they do not understand, and until they understand it, they cannot be released from it," he says.

How can I love that which has pained me gravely and taken away so much from me? I think of my parents, of Richard Wright, Claude Brown, Nikki Giovanni, Alice Walker, Wangari Maathai, Angela Davis, James Baldwin, and many more luminaries who seem to have found solace in doing the work without apology, remorse or vengeful intent. They have transcended the reactionary and intellectual barriers that hold me back from seeing the promises of tomorrow. They all seem to love deeply and profoundly.

At Oberlin College, one night, walking back to my dorm room, I send a whispered prayer into the universe: "I will love myself and everything that is me intensely and without apology."

Baldwin asks for self-love, an awareness of my profound humanity, and a sense of self-worth that holds no grudges. An affection that inspires and elevates one to a higher state of being. It is a transcendent kind of love. It forces all of us to investigate where and how we see ourselves and the conditions we find ourselves in. It is not by fate that we stand here. Fate, my brother Tee Ngugi had read somewhere, is not preordained. We are here, therefore, because of prescribed sets of circumstances set in motion by actors, some in good faith and with the best of intentions, some acting in deception and selfish interest, and others by their inactivity and acquiescence.

As I ponder my connection with the writings of James Baldwin at Oberlin College, I know that history will judge me harshly should I accept my lot in life and perish obscurely into the night. If history has taught me one thing, there are no innocent bystanders. In the words of my late mother, we cannot let them tear us apart.

*

The Fire is Now

When I come back from the store with a bag of flour, I frantically look for my mother. She owes me a story on Harlem.

"Well," she begins, "you see that poster of Sonia Sanchez in the office? 'Poem at Thirty'?" She pauses. "She handed it to your father and me at Fred Cartey's[1] apartment in New York. She read several of her poems to us that night."

I stare at her and imagine them all sitting on a stoop outside an apartment complex in Harlem, listening to Sonia. The moon is out over the New York of James Baldwin, the Harlem of the Renaissance, and the Black Arts Movement. I see my mother walking proudly amongst them. Black. Beautiful. And all I can ask is, "Was Baldwin there?"

---

1 Wilfred Cartey (1931-1992) was a literary critic and poet who taught at City College of New York and at Columbia University.

If Sonny's Blues were a song
it would sound something like this

Lola Oh

You have been thinking about jazz. Whether Baldwin heard the same rattle through the streets all those years ago. The cashier at the supermarket said you had trumpeter's hands

> You walk down Champs Elysées staring at the grooves in your palms. You've missed a call from your mom, sat opposite the fountain again watching pigeons dance

Dusk blankets the city until everything swimming under your eyelids is lilac,

The English swear too often, red faces clammy in the heat. You burn

> your tongue on an espresso, imagine yourself in a city with houses and windows

> that open outwards. The Eiffel Tower shrinks in the darkness, its stomach clutching

The police sirens choke the silence, you picture Giovanni in his sweaty apartment skin pale and tortured, aching for a man. You ride the metro, three stops to Opera

> fingers slick on the pole. You love the efficiency of this city. It's capacity to swallow things whole.

James Baldwin in Paris c. 1950s
Photographer unknown

Fahrenheit 1492

A Contraband Poem

Ewuare X. Osayande

"The victim who is able to articulate the situation
of the victim has ceased to be a victim:
he or she has become a threat."

— James Baldwin, *The Devil Finds Work*

Ok
We get it
I mean who would want their history such as yours taught?

when you consider what the record actually says
as recorded by your own writers, philosophers
who created the idea of race

trace the contours of history and what do we see?
except it's written by killers, conquistadors and enslavers
men who called themselves white
as right as to say superior

men who never would've imagined
that the people they put in chains
would ever be able to one day
read their captain's logs let alone their diaries

Fahrenheit 1492

but here we are
with the legacy of shame in today's terms
laid out plain

so yea, we get it

given your history of violence
such as it is
each page bleeding
with the guts of peoples from every corner of the globe
pilloried in the name of your privilege denied

would take a magic marker to your history
and mark it classified like the FBI
to hide all the dirt you've done

consider that
just about every world problem
began with a decision made by you
for the sake of brevity
we'll begin in 1492

who said white was so special?
that the rest of the world should worship you
as God?
sent missionaries around the world
to demonize our way of life
called us savages as you savaged our lands

Encounters with James Baldwin

when you teach your children to pray
you want them to imagine God as Santa Claus
who loves all the world that he gave his only son, begotten
not as the rotgut burner of women at the stake
not as the namesake blessed on the side of slave ships
not as the crucifiers of the Taino
who cut their babies in two
to test the sharpness of their blades.

you don't want them to know about Emmett Till
or thousands of Black people lynched
cause they might make the connection to
Trayvon Martin, Michael Brown, Sandra Bland, Breonna
Taylor, Philando Castile
and all the others unnamed
and come to you reeling from the sense of betrayal

but see
what you trying to do
ain't nothing new
our history been black-marketed since
you outlawed us learning
caught lashes on our back or worse
if caught with a book in hand
or when we stole ourselves free
from your plantations
as contraband
and crossed enemy lines during the war
that you still deny

Fahrenheit 1492

you fought to keep us enslaved
this is your brain on white supremacy
the disdain is palpable
it would be laughable
if it weren't true
got guns to the heads of teachers
daring them to tell the truth

ban books written by us
cause it hurts your brains
to read what terrible human beings
your fathers and mothers were and are

don't want your kids to see granny
spitting rabid at little Ruby Bridges
or the owner of America's team
smiling as his friends beat
Black kids integrating lunch counters in the South

you were good when all the books were written by you

whited out
Frederick Douglass, Nat Turner, and Sojourner Truth, Ida B.
Wells
lie about Pocahontas but erase Geronimo, Sitting Bull, and
Tecumseh
made mascots out of those you massacred
Colonized Puerto Rico, Hawaii, Guam, Haiti, Alaska, the
Philippines
Elvis Presleyed history

Encounters with James Baldwin

teach Thanksgiving
and tell us
the Indigenous just gave up their land
and walked onto reservations
willingly

published textbooks in Texas
teach we got in those ships ourselves
the chains were decorations
happy smiling darkies
"The Help"
not slaves
just "unpaid"
we volunteered our lives away
the whips were for our own good
like why you got us locked up in these 'hoods

or like when you banned the Chinese
from these shores
said they were like vermin
as in spreaders of disease
just like you tried to do after COVID-19

some of you cool with us learning about concentration camps
in Germany
not the ones here
that interned Japanese Americans for being Japanese
said it was National Security
like you do now with those who pray to the East

Fahrenheit 1492

ever uneased by identities you can't police
who live outside the confines you've manufactured
during the Dark Ages

there is no metaphor
more descriptive than you
in all your actual horror and filth

so what will you do?
burn books?
or burn the people you don't want writing them?

you see
when we called it a theory
that was just us playing nice

the fact is
ain't nothing theoretical about what has gone down

the fact is
there is no telling our story
without revealing you
as humanity's constant antagonist

the fact is we yawn at
your every pronouncement
of freedom and justice
as farcical
which is to say that

Encounters with James Baldwin

nobody believes that madness
except you

we see you for what you are

gaslight the whole world
and if that don't work
you'd set it on fire and
burn it out of spite

cause yours is a meritocracy of mediocrity

can't stand to see Black people happy
and you have the nerve to call us dysfunctional?
how many Black men been lynched
or murdered by cops
on account of a white woman
raised to lie with tears weaponized?

it is this very inheritance of arrogance
a blood privilege
passed down in willed estates of callousness
a sense of entitlement tied back
to family discussions and friendly bets
on who'll get to own the next "pickaninny"
born on the plantation
this for you is about more than books
it's about banning our lives
rendering us unread by the world

Fahrenheit 1492

judged by the cover of our skins

yet we are the text and testament
words walking in these tenements and barrios
each sacred as the next

we long done ripped ourselves
from your paper-thin script
the false narratives of your false consciousness
now unbound
we don't subscribe to your borders
live our lives beyond the pale
of your laws and legislation
giving perpetual side-eye to your sorry-ass ways

our truths
tis of We
are evidenced by every author
you despise and devise to ban
we been ever wise to you
as in hip or woke
after all, we come from the people
who said, "every shut eye ain't sleep"

but peep this
even when we couldn't read or write your words
we read you up and down
with a slow gaze of knowing
older than you

with eyes wide as the world
X-raying into your innards
with the effortless insight of Baldwin
incendiary as his eloquence
beating you with the intonations of a truth
that you still can't comprehend

you
who'd have us believe a lie
a lie as white and foul as your beliefs
as your violence wrapped in the coda of law
as your ignorance masquerading as value

but what we now know is that
every lie you have ever told
has come back in your face
as your own disgrace

how does it feel to be rendered naked
before the world
as a fraud?

call it white supremacy
when there's nothing supreme about you
at all

Passing

Nii Ayikwei Parkes

I discovered James Baldwin when I needed him, in a library in Reading, after a newspaper round on the same foldable green bike that I had ridden into a busy traffic intersection when I felt my father leave the earth. And because I encountered Baldwin when I needed him, I pass him on to people when I feel that they might need him.

I lost my father in the most violent way in 1994, just as I was learning to really appreciate him. I say violent not because there was a dramatic pile up of vehicles, from which his body was recovered after their burnt out carcasses were cleared, or because he fell from a roller coaster in the United States of America's deep south, looking – at each stilled millisecond of his fall – like he was being lynched, then gifted flight by gravity in a never-ending tussle between hatred and justice; I say violent because losing a parent is always violent, it's the ripping of a safety net from the edges of your world, making every move thereafter portentous. Stilling the storm of portent in my world was James Baldwin. Coming to the end of an Alice Walker marathon that had started while I was in Ghana, I was returning *The Temple of My Familiar* to the library when I saw a display – of Black authors – that included the collection of essays, *Nobody Knows My Name: More Notes of a Native Son* by James Baldwin. As I was wont to do at the time, I spent the day in the library reading from the essays, learning the art of unpacking Baldwin's long lines and gleaning the wisdoms woven into them. When the library closed, I left carrying his second novel, *Giovanni's Room*.

Encounters with James Baldwin

For all *Giovanni's Room*'s brilliance (and I had not really studied literature in any depth at the time; I was a science student, about to start a deferred science degree, who happened to love reading) what I connected with in the novel was David's alienation. I was, of course, struck by the fact that a 1950s novel written by an African American about white characters had been published, because even without knowing the publishing industry, it felt revolutionary. But ultimately, it was the alienation that resonated. I was a nineteen-year-old who had lost his father and could not adequately explain to anyone, not even his own family, the extent of his feelings of loss. Instead, I carried on in the world – working, smiling, having conversations, writing letters as David did to his father, without being honest – as if I had some sort of plan. I was adrift from the world.

I also held on to Baldwin because his essays carried and still carry more hope in the world than I have, and I desperately needed hope. To read Baldwin is to be drawn into his entreaties to white America and the optimism and generosity that underlies them. In many ways, I have learned from that spirit of generosity, without quite buying into the optimism; I have learned to forgive without necessarily expecting change to come from appealing to the goodness of others. Essentially, something passed over to me in my engagement with Baldwin, but not everything. I do not have his optimism, although I know that hope is foundational if we are to avoid despair. However, when despair approaches, I know where the optimism lives, I know to go to a Baldwin book to feel better – whether it's a play like *Blues for Mister Charlie*, which demonstrates that even in the midst of terror, we mimic, we laugh, we dance, or one of his scathing essays that still leave openings for embrace and rapprochement. I know how reading Baldwin makes me feel.

Why is this important? Well, at some point in teaching or mentoring, I tell writers whom I'm working with, "you'll feel it." That's because beyond offering some technical guidance and talking through social context and character development and genre expectations, at some point a writer has to lean into their storytelling with a degree of trust akin to faith, they have to be driven by the love of each character's peculiar language, they have to find a way to let the world they are creating become its full self, to beguile in the pitch of its own quirks. Nobody can teach how to hone that pitch, how to tune the story into song – you have to feel it. So, sometimes I offer a book to help navigate towards that feeling – often the book is a Baldwin book. I think, in hindsight, the reason why I pass Baldwin's work on is because whether the writing is sad, joyful, foreboding, reflective, playful, provocative, light or brooding, it is always uncomfortable – exactly the right degree of uncomfortable. Eavesdropping is uncomfortable, and I believe the best writing makes us feel like we are holding our ears to a wall, trying hard not to make a sound, so we can vicariously experience another world without being shut out. It is not possible to see Baldwin's generosity without facing the uncomfortable truths he articulates. When he writes in 'Letter from a Region in my Mind':

"It was absolutely clear that the police would whip you and take you in as long as they could get away with it [...] Neither civilized reason nor Christian love would cause any of those people to treat you as they presumably wanted to be treated; only the fear of your power to retaliate would cause them to do that, or to seem to do it, which was (and is) good enough [...] White people in this country will have quite enough to do in learning how to accept and love themselves and each other, and when they have achieved this – which will not be tomorrow and may very well be never – the Negro problem will no longer exist, for it will no longer be needed."

The generosity of his observation is not available to anyone unwilling to accept the truth of the painful discrimination, and the behaviours that the social milieu engenders. Without the discomfort, there is no learning, no progress.

Encounters with James Baldwin

In these distressing times we are living through, there is so much that is wrong that we can see – in the markets, in the environment, in the theatre of global politics and conflict. One would have to be blind not to see that the path that capitalism is willing us down leads to a world of selective light, where only the wealthiest, the most willing to exploit others, get to sit and enjoy sunsets. We have growing poverty, hopelessness, starvation, homelessness, discrimination, gender-based violence, xenophobia; we have people who know they are ill, but are choosing not to access healthcare because it is so expensive that they would have to trade off their daily needs in order to afford medical treatment; and we have a range of conflicts in Congo, Sudan, Palestine, Ethiopia, which are clearly about financial gain, from which we are constantly being distracted by elaborate smoke screens. Every one of these things I have listed is covered in James Baldwin's 1979 article in *The Nation*, when he speaks of his Christian faith and how it remains a compass for him, even though he is no longer a preacher or living under the roof of a preacher:

"I was instructed to feed the hungry, clothe the naked and visit those in prison. I am far indeed from my youth, and from my father's house, but I have not forgotten these instructions, and I pray upon my soul that I never will."

Since the nations that lead the propagation of capitalism are, almost without exception, so-called Christian nations, one might ask why their leaders do not possess the same zeal as Baldwin, why even in their own countries, they are so resistant to feeding the hungry, caring for the sick, clothing the naked, and attending to the imprisoned. Beyond that, why don't the citizens of those countries rise up and demand that their leaders live up to these ideals? The answer lies in the feeling I try to pass on when I gift a Baldwin book – discomfort. The real opiate of capitalism is comfort, it is the drug that blinds, that stunts learning, that cripples empathy and the entryway drug is convenience. I have, now and then, joked that the more one visits a convenience store, the less prepared one is for revolution. Frantz Fanon puts it another way:

"What matters today, the issue which blocks the horizon, is the need for a redistribution of wealth."

That reality is a very uncomfortable matter for any nations whose wealth is founded on the colonisation of other nations. It is a sensitive topic for their leaders and awkward for their citizens. Once one has some kind of income, some measure of comfort, the question that precedes any action, any request or quest for justice is: will this inconvenience the source of my income? Will I be able to support the people who depend on me? So, ultimately, the people who shout for justice, are the ones with nothing to lose – or those who do not yet have responsibility for anyone but themselves. This is why students are often at the forefront of protests, students and the wretched of the earth: the formerly colonised, formerly enslaved, survivors of abuse, the marginalised who have not yet been drawn into the embrace of comfort.

James Baldwin's power derives from the fact that he never knew comfort. He was denied a childhood because he had to help raise his much younger siblings, he was a minority in his high school because of his brilliance; he was Black, queer, occasionally an alien (in France and in the American South), an introvert in very public spaces, outspoken in a world that required silence from Black folk, and in the end committed to joy in a world that is largely a den of misery. Discomfort is the periphery of things, but the periphery also gives a wide view. In the same *The Nation* article of September 1979 – 'Open Letter to the Born Again' – he asserts very clearly that: "… the state of Israel was not created for the salvation of the Jews; it was created for the salvation of the Western interests."

How obvious is that becoming in today's world, stemming from events that have escalated almost exactly forty-five years since he published the article? Yes, it was uncomfortable when he wrote it and it will be uncomfortable for several powerful people now, but, as always, it was written with a spirit of generosity, already making a distinction between Judaism and Zionism at a time when many people were not. It is this combination of sharpness and tenderness that has meant that I have bought *The Fire Next Time*, *Giovanni's Room*, *Nobody Knows My Name* and *Go Tell It on the Mountain* over a dozen times, but I always struggle to find a copy in my house – I lend or give them away with such regularity and the lent copies rarely come back. This is how Baldwin never passes; he gets passed on.

In 2019, I had a wide-ranging discussion with Angolan artist and activist Nástio Mosquito and I opened up about how, while I had come to terms with the loss of my father, I sometimes still wanted the comfort of his presence, his own voice saying what I already know he would say. I released that excerpt of the conversation as a standalone recording called *What Alone Means*. At this time in the world, I feel like that about Baldwin too. I believe I know exactly what he would say, but I would love to hear him say it in his inimitable voice, delivered with authority, with urgency, with wide-eyed conviction, with deep-rooted generosity, but uncomfortable – to lean into more current lingo – AF. For this is no time for comfort. It's time to pass from comfort to radical alertness. It's Baldwin time.

"Trust life, and it will teach you, in joy and sorrow, all you need to know."

– James Baldwin

James Baldwin in his house in Saint Paul de Vence.
Photo: Office de tourisme, Saint Paul de Vence

James Baldwin and Anton Phillips in 1987
Photo: fantompowa.net

The Amen Corner[1]

Anton Phillips

My connection with James Baldwin was to produce his play *The Amen Corner* at the Tricycle Theatre, which later transferred to the West End of London. How this came about is really quite interesting.

I arrived in England in about 1963, and one of the things I had with me was a copy of his play, *The Amen Corner* (1954) which I travelled with from America back to Jamaica, back to America, and then finally to England. It was with me all the time. Twenty-five years later, I managed to get to produce the play at The Tricycle Theatre in Kilburn (now The Kiln). I had the cast – Carmen Munroe, Clarke Peters, and various other people. I had the money courtesy of the London Arts Board. I had the theatre courtesy of Nick Kent at The Tricycle. What I didn't have were the rights to the play and tracking those down was difficult because you go through the usual channels and nobody knew who held the rights to the play. Anyway, someone suggested that I speak to the film director, Horace Ové, so I called Horace and he gave me Mr Baldwin's number in the South of France. I telephoned and someone answered. I said, "Hello, may I speak to Mr James Baldwin?" The response was, "This is he."

I explained what I wanted and he was really interested. I said, "Can I come and see you and talk about it?" He said,

1 An edited version of the speech given by Anton Phillips at the unveiling of a blue plaque in honour of James Baldwin on May 17th, 2024, at Hackney CVS, which Baldwin visited in 1985 when it was a library. The plaque was installed by Nubian Jak and Black History Walks.

"Yes." So, I ran downstairs from my office to the nearest travel agent and managed to get a ticket for Nice in a couple of days' time. I went back up and called him and said, "I'll be in Nice on Friday." When I arrived in Nice, there was James Baldwin at the airport waiting to meet me. We went to his house just outside Nice, in Saint Paul de Vence. But a beautiful country house, a farmhouse up in the hills. The smell of wild thyme all around; a great location. I spent the weekend there and we talked about life, the universe, everything. And of course, *The Amen Corner*.

When the play was finally in rehearsal, he came over to England for the last week of rehearsals, so he was accessible to the cast. And we spent a lot of time together. We dined frequently but we never spoke about anything heavy, like politics.

His visit to London was invaluable because it gave us publicity which money couldn't buy. The play was hugely successful. It transferred to the West End of London, and he came back again for that and made himself available for even more publicity: television interviews, newspaper interviews, magazines, and so on. Again, publicity, which people would die for – anybody producing a play would.

It was fascinating because *The Amen Corner* is also partly autobiographical like *Go Tell It on the Mountain*. He'd come into the theatre at night, stand in the back and just look at the stage, and you could see on his face, sort of him going back in time and looking at those people on stage, and putting himself in that situation in Harlem from the days when he was heavily involved in the church with his family.

The thing that really is striking about James Baldwin is when you got to know him, and it didn't take long, you felt that you'd known this person all your life. He was that sort of person – you immediately warmed to him, and he made you feel that he knew you and you could talk to him. You didn't have to be in awe of him or anything like that. When you were in his company, it didn't take long before you called him Jimmy. And it was, "Jimmy, let's go have a drink."

Well, in fact, I never said that to him because I was told, "Don't get him drinking!"and "Don't let his cronies capture him when he is here in London and lead him astray." So we tried to keep a tight bow on him while he was here.

He stayed with Clarke Peters. Clarke, of course, is a very well-known singer and actor. When Clarke first came to Europe, he went to Paris. He was busking on the streets of Paris. And as Clarke has described it, he saw this little man across the street studying him who came over. It turned out that it was James Baldwin. Clarke explained that he was busking to get some money to go to Holland to do a gig there. James Baldwin said to him, "Well, how much do you need?" And he gave him the money. And then he said, "Well, what about when you're there? I mean, do you have money for accommodation?" And he gave him some more money. And that was the first connection that they had. So, it was great that when James came to London for *The Amen Corner,* that he was able to stay with Clarke.

My abiding memory of James Baldwin is a man of great humour. He was very funny. Perhaps he was a little cynical by then because I think the death of Martin Luther King Jr affected him greatly. But he was someone who I remember with immense fondness, not only for his work, but just as a wonderful, warm, human being.

A Higher Calling

Ray Shell

I must have been fourteen or fifteen years old when I first read James Baldwin's *Go Tell It on the Mountain,* this iconic missive resonated with me on so many levels and for so many reasons. It was the cultural and especially the spiritual links I shared with 'King James' that immediately glued me to the literary life of John Grimes, the protagonist of the story.

John's father, Gabriel, was his stepfather and a pastor of the church the Grimes family attended, just as my father, Charles Shell, was my stepfather and a pastor of the Pentecostal church the Shell family attended. All of Baldwin's Pentecostal iconography, rituals and imagery resonated powerfully within me. I understood and experienced first-hand the dark secrets of John Grimes' tainted revelations. I too had felt the 'spirit coming down' in the midst of the church Saints, dressed in their 'Blood Of The Lamb' white robes… I too had witnessed and watched the Saints whirling under the power of the Holy Ghost, prophesying and 'Speaking in Tongues'… I too had struggled with carnal thoughts that strayed darkly away from the Holy Straight And Narrow Thoughts of the Saved And Sanctified Community of which, at age thirteen, I became a member.

The life Baldwin described in *Go Tell It on the Mountain*, his first novel, was my life so I instinctively knew James Baldwin was someone I could trust, learn from and emulate, that he wrote and created visceral stories of truth based on his living experiences in our Black American Ghetto meant I could do the same thing, so, by using him as a 'mirror' of inspiration, I honour 'King James' by trying to write words of simple clarity and irrefutable power just as he did.

I don't remember actively hoping to ever meet 'King James'. I didn't believe it was possible as I understood he didn't live in the United States, so when I was brought to the United Kingdom by Oscar Johnson and Lon Satton to star in a West End gospel musical and met my stage brother, Clarke Peters, who was also starring in the West End production of *Bubbling Brown Sugar*, I was intrigued when he told me that he'd met Baldwin in Paris when he first arrived in Europe and how Baldwin had mentored him. I felt like I was a few steps closer to the 'King' even though, as I said, I wasn't actively searching for him.

I started reading his collection of essays, *The Fire Next Time,* and I realized then that Baldwin was more than just a novelist – he was a chronicler of Black African American thought, and an activist with political ideas that I agreed with. He was not afraid to question the agenda of white America, nor to question America's commitment to Black people, which is something I also questioned but had never spoken about publicly. I had never put any thoughts down on paper about this, but the fact that James Baldwin *did* write about the state of Black people in white America in every book he wrote, in every television, magazine or newspaper interview he appeared in, made me realize that Baldwin was more than a conventional novelist. 'King James' had a Higher Calling like that of the boy preacher he'd been before he took up the pen, a Higher Calling anointed by God. That it was possible for artists to be more than entertainers or court jesters panhandling for public acceptance and financial validation, meant it was possible we could produce, like Baldwin, sacred texts containing uncomfortable truths that admirers and critics could either agree with or vehemently disavow. The important thing was, James Baldwin was *not* afraid to put what he thought and felt on paper for the entire world to see.

Encounters with James Baldwin

I've lived in the UK since 1978, my children and grandchildren were born here, and the knowledge that James Baldwin felt more at home outside of America resonated with me as well. When I came to this country in 1978, I immediately realized the UK could be a haven for me. I appreciated the relative calm and safety in West London that was the opposite to what was happening in South Ozone Park, Queens, where I'd come from. Guns and drug violence were terrifying features of my American life in New York City. There were no guns here. I was a father of two girls and my then wife (celebrity chef Momma Cherri) and I were not gun-carrying 'hood rats so we felt safer here as we didn't have to look behind our backs every time we ventured into the streets. After growing up and dealing with the negative drama that was inherent in New York City, living in London was a piece of cake.

Reading how 'King James' felt about living outside of the United States and learning about the United States from Europe was another big, resonating connection. After reading *Giovanni's Room*,[1] Baldwin's second novel, I recognized the Higher Calling in his writing with his diversity of characters and story ideas. *Giovanni's Room* was a universal story instead of a Black story and I connected with that as well. I viewed Madonna with different eyes when I learned that she once owned (might still own) the film rights to *Giovanni's Room*.

I finally met James Baldwin in 1985 when Lon Satton who was starring with me in *Starlight Express* invited James Baldwin to see the show and afterwards brought him to my dressing room and introduced us. It was a brief visit and I was mouth-agape starstruck. I hadn't published anything and wouldn't have dared to speak to him about writing because I didn't consider myself a writer at the time.

'King James' said the most wonderful things about my

1 It wasn't seen as a Black novel and Knopf, his publisher, threatened to burn it because they feared its subject of homosexual love would turn off his core Black readership.

performance. He signed something for me and before he left, he said, "You put the star in *Starlight Express…*" I was thrilled. Thrilled to have actually met this master of words and a mentor. I have two writing mentors, one man, one woman, both Black: James Baldwin and Maya Angelou. Maya Angelou anointed my debut novel *ICED*. She gave me a blurb that opened literary doors for me and *ICED* exists and took inspiration from the writing of James Baldwin.

Now that I am a published author, I wish Baldwin was still living, as I'd love to have a conversation with him about his essay 'Down At The Cross' from *The Fire Next Time*. He opens his essay with a quote from Kipling's poem 'Take Up the White Man's Burden' and a verse from 'Down At The Cross', a Baptist hymn; both are apropos. In his essay, Baldwin rages against the inhumanity the white man has inflicted on the Black man in America and gives a scathing report card of how white America disregards the existence of the American Negro, as we were called then. Baldwin says: "The universe which is not merely the stars and the moon and the planets, flowers, grass and trees, but *other people,* has evolved no terms for your existence, has made no room for you, and if love will not swing wide the gates, no other power will or can." The universe Baldwin cites is the white universe in which we Blacks do not exist.

'King James' also explains why he left the church. He could not reconcile the white man's God of Love with the white man's machinations against the Black man since the day we arrived in chains on American shores:

"If the concept of God has any validity or any use, it can only be to make us larger, freer, and more loving. If God cannot do this, then it is time we got rid of Him." Baldwin was unequivocal on the subject of God and his allowance of Black suffering in White America.

Baldwin's conversation with the Honorable Elijah Muhammad was illuminating. He admitted to being afraid to accept a dinner invitation from Muhammad, "I was frightened, because I had, in effect, been summoned into a royal presence. I was frightened for another reason [... they] knew more about me, and had read more of what I had written, than I had expected, and I wondered what they made of it all."

Baldwin knew Muhammad wanted him onside as an ally. He had a large platform, a huge following and as an ally of the Nation of Islam, 'King James' could be very useful. Although he understood the dogma and politics of Elijah Muhammad, he would not join the Nation of Islam. "'I left the church twenty years ago and I haven't joined anything since.' It was my way of saying that I did not intend to join their movement either [...] I'm a writer. I like doing things alone."

Baldwin didn't hate enough to be in the Nation of Islam, he didn't consider all whites as devils and he didn't think the Nation's plan of segregating themselves in the seven states they felt the US government should gift to Black Americans would solve their economic issues. He believed the American government would never give up that land and that having a separate economy outside of the United States would not deliver the billions of dollars that Elijah Muhammad thought it would to Black people.

I'm grateful we do have James Baldwin's words. Those words are needed now when people of colour all around the globe are finally understanding that poverty has no colour, and that power concentrated in the hands of a few is not a just or fair way to run society, and it's time to change it. I believe 'King James' would be proud of the global student protests taking place on campuses today in the name of fairness, freedom and solidarity – subjects which James Baldwin believed in and fiercely wrote about.

"*This is the charged, the dangerous moment, when everything must be re-examined, must be made new, when nothing at all can be taken for granted.*"

– **James Baldwin**

For Jimmy

SuAndi

During my career I have been lucky to have met many esteemed people who through their art have pushed hard against the barriers of racism, performing with artists such as Jalal Mansur Nuriddin and Umar Bin Hassan (The Last Poets) and Amiri Baraka. But what really informed me were the opportunities I had to listen to experiences way beyond my own. I am not saying we hung out together, but Baraka would share his thoughts while we were together in Atlanta, North Carolina, and New York. I had a few phone chats with Maya Angelou and how my chest would swell with pride whenever Dick Gregory invited me to join his breakfast table while at the National Black Theatre Festival in North Carolina. But Jimmy, I had to read your words, and in the beginning, I didn't really comprehend what you were detailing before me.

I had followed my brother, Malcolm, into books whose titles were made accessible by prison librarians in their attempt to appease, and possibly contain, incarcerated Black men. Yet, as I worked my way through *Soledad Brother* and *Soul on Ice,* even though the news increasingly screened the brutality that the civil rights movement and the Black Panthers faced daily, I was living in the fantasy world of British tolerance. The 1919 lynching of Charles Wootton was not to be exposed until many years later, so, the news I watched on the small black and white TV screen was of a racial bigotry and brutality not existing in the UK. But as history is my favourite subject, how did I manage to overlook the British colonisation of America in 1587 and its role in the Slave Trade?

I had been raised on Keats. Forced to memorise his words

so much that I can on occasion repeat a line or two even now. But his voice hurt my soul and even though I was in England, the imagery his writing brought forth seemed alien to me. I was growing in maturity, I needed voices to soothe me, to understand my increasing struggles as I became more and more aware of the blockades strategically placed before me to prevent my progress in life as a Black woman, as a Black writer developing her cultural, social and political awareness.

I first met you in *Giovanni's Room;* please allow me the cliché "most of my male friends were gay." Still, I am not sure I truly understood the need for their shame and secrecy. Yes, I would sometimes play the girlfriend, especially for Black men at a time when HIV was still lingering in the shadows. I "enjoyed" the book while largely failing to comprehend the lives in danger.

You once wrote: "You think your pain and your heartbreak are unprecedented in the history of the world, but then you read." It was books, you said, "that taught me that the things that tormented me most were the very things that connected me with all the people who were alive, who had ever been alive."[1]

My friends had begun to die

Years later, older and hopefully wiser, I took my seat in a lecture theatre full of Black people. Two pasty-faced academics were researching the cinema tastes of different demographics. They were visibly nervous and mentioned that in the other sessions, each group had independently picked their favourite film, whereas we were not given that option. Then spluttering, they tried to find the courage to advise us that the film contained certain language that might offend us. Someone asked, "what in particular?" The two men turned to each other hesitantly, hoping the other would reply. Almost in one voice the room chanted, "Nigger, nigger, nigger!", and then we laughed at their discomfort.

1 James Baldwin, 'The Doom and Glory of Knowing Who You Are', *Life Magazine,* May 24, 1963.

As it turned out we were to watch you in a documentary film that had never been on general release. There you were at The West Indian Student Centre, London, UK, filmed by the late great Horace Ové. We watched in silence, almost... aside from when we laughed in agreement even though the topic was hard to take in its reality, and some of us whispered "Yes, yes."

Personally, I was grateful to those pasty-faced men who had organised the evening for the chance to watch you in action.

You were signifying we understood, they didn't.

There must be countless writers who have committed themselves to the statement that you made them the writer they are today. I can't say that because to do so would not just be egotistical of me, but also to lay my failures on you too.

What your words did is educate me beyond the national myths of British heroes and the symbol of the 'White Cliffs of Dover,' and beyond the glorification of the history books (*sic*) telling of the amazing feats of the white man. I learnt how their demonic behaviour had infested our psyche, particularly our men, making so many feel useless in their maleness and their inability to achieve and provide for their families. Yet still, no matter how much they glorified the past, and how far they have been prepared to go to dehumanise Black folk, we have come through and managed to survive. Not without setbacks, sometimes colossal ones, such as the loss of Brother Martin Luther King Jr. We started and continue the Long March for equality and human rights brought to worldwide attention by Brother Martin. To quote you: "Your crown has already been bought and paid for. All you must do is put it on"[2]

The tension Brother Malcolm's words created had for some time wallpapered my home with a white mother at its head. They needed to be studied and analysed to go beyond the anger that we felt at the deprivation we had suffered. That

2 James Baldwin, *The Price of the Ticket,* New York: St Martin's Press, 1985.

our heroes had been labelled criminal. That it is our collective intellect that will keep on pushing through and in doing so, my brother, Malcolm, known locally as Assassin, learnt the value of Sankofa and the need to retrieve our African history.

Today I see England with different eyes. Sadly, I am often clumsy because the enemy does not always have blue eyes. The iris of compassion comes in all shades. That equality does not mean we get to live in the house of our enemies – we have to build our own. That the sexual abuse of enslaved Africans still masks itself in homophobia. We are not yet perfect. I doubt we will ever be.

> I wonder if those in your time frame
> Honoured you
> Did the men who loved women
> On their front porch privacy
> Let slip from mouths slit sideways
> Speak of you in brotherhood
> Or resent your wisdom
> For you lived outside
> Their experience of loving
> Despite the risk to your living[3]

But truth has to be the first line we write in fact or fiction. Because our stories, lives, history have been cloaked in a conspiracy of white supremacy. "People are trapped in history and history is trapped in them"[4]

Times have changed, Jimmy, but the world today is far from perfect. On both sides of the Golden Pond the death toll of our Black brothers and sisters is horrifying. Many have fallen.

Many slain by the so-called forces of justice, which are not accountable for the number of their murders.

*

3 SuAndi 2024.
4 James Baldwin, *Notes of a Native Son,* Boston: Beacon Press, 1955.

I would have loved to have sat with you and watched you reaching for a cigarette as you spoke. I wonder if you would have found my view of life as naïve from the aspect of tolerance that England likes to show to the outside world. Or would you find me a revolutionary taking risks as I push for respect and equality? I hope the latter. But had you been able to live forever, it would have meant you would have had to witness all those you love, die.

> "Life is tragic simply because the earth turns and the sun
> inexorably rises and sets, and one day, for each of us,
> the sun will go down for the last, last time."[5]

5 James Baldwin, *The Fire Next Time,* New York: Dial Press, 1963.

Wherefore, Nuncle?

Tade Thompson

I saw a TV show in the pre-pandemic era. I don't remember its name. It was late at night, and I remember it was set in France, maybe Paris. This kid, barely eighteen, was trying to raise money to pay for his mother's Hajj trip to Mecca. They were not well off. The entire episode was about the shenanigans in service of acquiring money that ensued.

And yet, in their possession was a book, *The Price of the Ticket,* by one James Baldwin. I checked. At the time of that show, the book cost £1400.00. It's come down now, especially with the Library of America editions, but what struck me is how they had something of value that could solve their problems but didn't investigate it. I often feel that way about Baldwin's essays. I feel that because we have them in plain sight, we don't value them nearly as much as we should. Yet each one remains as potent and relevant as they were when first published.

How does one write about James Baldwin? He said everything he wanted to say about himself, and a thousand undergrads and postdocs have vacuumed up and picked over what is left. But what does James Baldwin mean to me? The best way to put it is that Baldwin gave me *permission*. Permission to disagree, permission to think, and permission to have my own rage, which allowed me to reject or at least examine what I can only describe as a pervasive expectation of mediocrity and acquiescence.

In my teen years, I saw his words here and there, of course. How could I not? Always a favourite in books of quotations.

Encounters with James Baldwin

Reading these offcuts, stripped of context like literary orphans, I thought, to my shame, that he was white, and my reaction was always, "Hmm, I never thought of it that way," and I'd move on to something else. Later, in university, I discovered a transcript of his Cambridge Union debate with William F. Buckley of 1965, and I decided this was an intellectual to know, after which I encountered him in context by borrowing two of his books from the library – *Notes of a Native Son* and *The Fire Next Time*.

Reading Baldwin was the first time I felt a clear and incisive mind. I had never known writing like this. In my teens, I felt myself elevated by every single essay of his, and I still do today. To walk through the world was to wade through an intellectual sludge, which, to me, worked in the interest of the ruling classes. Vagueness and uncertainty hiding behind confidently deployed jargon and obfuscation was and is the order of the day. Baldwin gave me the language to describe my experience, and the attitude to counter it.

I kept wondering, how does he do it? To write clearly, one must think clearly. And to think clearly one must observe accurately and form the correct connections between precepts. In my youth, every book was written for my own edification. Solipsistic necessity, you understand. Baldwin did all that work for me to emulate.

There is a British term, a verb, *to monster*, which means to reprimand. Baldwin was a monsterer. He also gave warnings, which is interesting, considering the root of the word 'monster' is 'to warn' or 'portent'. I often play a mental game with the news cycle. What would Baldwin have made of the Black Lives Matter movement? Of Trump? Of Barack Obama? Instead of What Would Jesus Do? I play the mental game – 'What Would Baldwin Say?' He was harsh, but he could also be self-aware, and express regret at early actions, as evidenced in his memoir/eulogy for Richard Wright, with whom he fell out over his essay, 'Everybody's Protest Novel'. Wright thought Baldwin had betrayed all African Americans in general, and him in particular, by taking aim at the protest novel. He contended that Baldwin had used criticism of *Native Son* to launch his career as a writer. Baldwin spared nobody, white, Black, Brown – it didn't matter. Everybody went under the microscope of his intellect, and he was fearless.

Being gay gave Baldwin a double-dip of discrimination in the US at a time when homosexuality was generally closeted. My father, a lawyer, introduced me to a lot of 'canonical' thinkers, but never mentioned Baldwin. Or Audre Lorde, come to think of it. It was definitely not an oversight. The more I think of it, the more I conclude that the obstacle was Queerness. To read Baldwin is to understand that African Americans were, at the time, taught to be ashamed of everything African about them – from their physical appearance to the idea that Africa contributed nothing to human civilisation, through to the absence of heroes to look up to. Maybe this is why his mind ranged from his own position to the African American experience generally, seen in the context of African geopolitics and the protean white reactions to a rapidly changing social landscape.

How does one negotiate such rage? How do you translate it from post-war Harlem to Lambeth where I was living as a child? What are the parallels, and do the truisms still apply?

The Cold War that Baldwin was immersed in played out differently in Africa, and there was nothing cold about it. We burned in the heat of it, in Angola, in the various iterations of the Congo, and in Nigeria. More than once, I've described the Cold War as a shooting war in Africa, and when I read the essay, 'East River, Downtown', I saw Baldwin put "cold" in parenthesis. I had a visceral reaction. Of course I couldn't have been the only one who thought this, but nobody was saying it in my circle. He noted that for the Black person to be communist or socialist may have had less to do with a philosophical disagreement with capitalism, and more to do with the desire to be treated as equal to other human beings. Not brutalised, not equated to a beast, and not infantilised, like the West of the Cold War era was wont to do.

Veneration is easy when the venerated are no longer a threat. The mainstream recognises our intellectuals as trouble-makers until they're dead, when they become heroes after literal and metaphorical martyrdom. Thus to Black thought leaders, acknowledged only when de-fanged by the grave.

Thus to James Baldwin.

White people think of these matters as either academic or some situation where the appropriate emotion is pity or tut-tutting. Some may, in a fit of liberal ecstasy, protest. For those of us who are Black, however, it is a matter of avoiding death and dehumanising conditions, a matter of the quality of day-to-day life, a matter of survival.

Black people do not need a James Baldwin to understand prejudice or the dangers of living while Black. That's our lived experience. But Baldwin gives a language with which to scream it out into the void of indifference. The ability to elucidate the nuances of our lives is what will help end it, even if, at the time of writing, that seems hopelessly out of view.

Then comes responsibility to the coming generation. How do I tell my children and nieces and nephews about Baldwin in a way that stokes curiosity? All this in an age of 280 characters swimming in AI swill masquerading as convenience. I imagine them staring at me as I offer *Notes of a Native Son* for a birthday gift. Wherefore, Nuncle? What reason for deep thought in the internet age?

Baldwin understood, but more importantly, he could express what it means to be Black in a non-Black world. And so, what I take from him and his work, is that I must spare no one, I must last, and I must get my work done. When the unpleasant and the grotesque occurs, I must not look away. I must look closer and bring what I see to those who cannot or will not look. As aspirations go, I can think of nothing better.

Whether there be civil war, natural disaster, pogroms, or nuclear Armageddon, I will live and die in the world I wake up in, but thanks to Baldwin, I will describe that world with clear language and intentionality.

Letter to My Brother

Ruminations and reflections of my trip
to London

Patrick Vernon

*This is an imaginary letter from James Baldwin to his
younger brother David reflecting on his visit to the CLR
James Library in Dalston, Hackney in July 1985 and events
that occurred in the months after that.*

Dear David,

How are you and the family? Sorry it's taken a while to write
to you. The last few months have been quite exhausting pre-
paring for the publication of *The Evidence of Things Not Seen*.
As you know, it's based on the essay I did back in 1981 looking
at the Atlanta child murders. Thankfully, it's had some initial
positive reviews, so it might begin to sell.

I have been reflecting a lot on life and especially about con-
serving my energy after spending this time last year in hospital
for exhaustion. I really appreciate your support as always being
there for me! Although I feel better, I'm still tired and not
feeling a hundred per cent myself. I've decided I will do only
one more semester teaching at UMass so I can focus on my
writing and enjoy the beauty of the Côte d'Azur. Of course,
the publishers are still putting pressure on me to complete the
book about Medgar, Martin, and Malcolm but it's difficult to
write about them and how much we have lost. It's tragic that
all three were assassinated by the Republic and I can't bear
to think about how they deliberately killed off our leadership,

great men in their prime. In a strange way, this will strengthen us and one day we are going to run Capitol Hill. I'm going to persevere, as we did back in the day when our people were sent out to work in the cotton fields, head down just to complete my first draft. I need the money as I want to buy my home in Saint Paul de Vence. I just love this place. I've been here now for so many years, it's where I can rest and find solace – that's still a revolutionary act for a Black man, as Audre used to remind me all the time! I've negotiated with the landlady to buy the property by instalments. Who knows, you may be able to help me, David. I know that you'll love this place too when you come over to see me.

Anyway, on a positive note, I spent a lovely time in July in London. I was there to do a number of things. I met up with a potential producer who wants to stage my play *The Amen Corner* next year in the West End, which is like Broadway. If it comes off, it will be the first production there with an all-Black cast, which will be a big deal for England. I also went to a place called Dalston in the Borough of Hackney (reminds me of Harlem in the early 1970s) where there is a significant Black population of migrants from Africa and the Caribbean.

I was invited as the guest of honour by activists and librarians who have been campaigning for more Black literature in the libraries in Hackney, where they have an anti-racist approach to education, housing and the arts. It was held at the CLR James Library, named after my great friend. I remember meeting his nephew, Darcus Howe, who is a well-known activist and former Black Panther leader, as well as a writer and publisher of *Race Today,* a radical campaigning magazine which brings together all people of colour to fight racism and achieve liberation there.

Being in London I felt I was in a time capsule, back witnessing the civil rights movement in the 1960s. I never saw myself as a leader! But you have to witness, record and share the stories of the Black struggle or the so-called "Negro problem." Britain's got a Negro problem too! It is a problem linked to its history of slavery and empire. I learned a lot about Britain in my conversations in the library. They talked about the *Windrush,* apparently this was the name of a ship that was originally in the German fleet during the Second World War. How ironic! I guess in years to come *Windrush* and the people who travelled in her will be a by-word for post-war Black migration to England's shores.

Their migration story is similar to the journeys our ancestors made from the American deep South to Northern cities. The differences are that people are coming from countries or colonies which were once part of Britain and her empire. The right to citizenship seems arbitrary depending on which political party is in power. They have a right-wing leader named Margaret Thatcher, similar to Ronald Reagan. Actually, they are friends. I saw a poster for the film *Gone with the Wind* in a radical bookshop the other day which featured them as the actors Vivien Leigh and Clark Gable! The poster was about stopping the proliferation of nuclear weapons which, as a long-standing pacifist, I found amusing. Reagan is no Gary Cooper or John Wayne, but I guess he now has the world as his stage in protecting white supremacy! There is an amazing group of women camped at Greenham Common too; they've occupied a RAF base that the Republic uses to stockpile horrific weapons. Britain is almost like another state of America, its poodle, in the so-called 'special relationship.' I'm sure the ghosts of the *Mayflower* or the Boston Tea Party will be laughing in their graves, seeing how the Republic is controlling the old country. It's becoming too much like America in the way it treats Black people so I wouldn't live there.

I sensed the fear that Black people have there. I've read about the violence of the police against the miners who were striking to protect their livelihoods, so what chance does the Black man have to survive and thrive? The same dehumanisation and degradation of Black people goes on, despite all the white liberal rhetoric of anti-racism and equality.

It's not quite as bad as it was when I first went down to the deep South in America, but there's still fear. The far-right parties like the National Front are a threat, being given permission by Margaret Thatcher's rhetoric to instil more fear and enact racial violence. The police seem to be part of the problem, just like our own police back in the Republic. They recently shot a mother, Cherry Groce, in a place called Brixton which has a large Black community and Colin Roach, a young Black man died mysteriously of a gunshot wound whilst at a notorious police station in Stoke Newington. There was rioting too at Broadwater Farm, a deprived social housing project, where a police officer was killed by Black youth. It feels like the fire has come back again, with uprisings in London and the North of England where Black communities are fighting for their survival, fighting to be heard. So, we still have a lot to do.

It's funny how much people in London love all my writing from the 1960s and 70s. I'm sure there will be a time when Black and white will unite. Not in the same way as we did during the civil rights movement, but there's a possibility. Martin was able to bring together white people, Black people, Jews and Gentiles, under the banner of civil rights. I can imagine in years to come Black and white uniting together, recognising inequalities, racism, discrimination. Maybe the time will come when white people will value and respect us, our history, our culture, and our humanity, and give us the chance to rest and thrive.

Whilst there's unrest, there's a cool arts and culture scene in London with writers, filmmakers, artists, musicians, academics, and fashion designers shaping a new aesthetic around Black British culture and identity which reminds me of the Harlem Renaissance. At the heart of this is a growing Black gay scene too where spaces and clubs are being established, something I wish we'd had back in the day in Harlem.

David, there's so much to say, but I'm tired, really tired. I've got to finish this damn book but I haven't got the energy and I can't seem to get over the loss of Malcolm, Martin and Medgar not even reaching the age of forty … I'm lucky, I suppose, I'm still here at sixty-one and I'm still writing. But I can't help wondering if people still respect the work I'm doing? I know you do. And it meant a lot when people like Toni Morrison, Maya Angelou, Tony Cade Bambara all came to visit me here – and of course, Miles Davis. They all love and praise my writing. But in America, do they really value my work? Who knows? Maybe when I'm dead and gone, they might recognise that, as a witness, I've been able to communicate the experiences of hurt and discrimination that Black people have faced. Who knows? Am I being a bit morbid? Feeling sorry for myself? Maybe I'm drinking too much Scotch as I write this letter?!

By the way, I almost forgot to tell you my big news. I've just received a letter from the government here. The president, François Mitterrand, has invited me to receive a Legion of Honour award next year. It's one of the highest accolades they give to a foreign national. It's really fantastic. David, if you're free, please come over to the award ceremony in Paris next January. It'll mean so much to me if you can be there to join me.

Take care. Your brother,

Jamie

November 1985
St Paul de Vence

James Baldwin and Black British Civil Rights

Tony Warner

James Baldwin (centre) visiting the CLR James Library in Hackney in 1985.
Photo: Hackney CVS/www.hackney.gov.uk.

If you mention the term 'civil rights' to the average British person, there is an automatic default to the civil rights era in America, with the names of Rosa Parks, Martin Luther King and Angela Davis often referenced. Yet, there was a parallel struggle against white supremacy in Britain in the same period. Racial discrimination was widespread and normalised in the fields of education, housing, healthcare, banking and policing.

Encounters with James Baldwin

It was not until 1965, decades after groups like Dr Harold Moody's 1930s League of Coloured Peoples had demanded legal equality, and centuries after racism had been embedded in society by British slavery, that the first Race Relations Act was passed in the UK. The Act, "banned racial discrimination in public places and made the promotion of racial hatred on the grounds of 'colour, race, or ethnic or national origins' an offence." That fairly weak law was followed by further Acts in 1968, 1976, 2000, and 2010 to strengthen the protections against racism.

Through his frequent visits to the UK, James Baldwin became part of this Black British history. In 1968, Baldwin and Dick Gregory, whose book *N: An Autobiography*, had been published by a London publisher in 1965, spoke at the West Indian Students Centre in Earls Court (WISC). The venue was a hotbed of revolutionary learning and political activity. Their visit was filmed by Trinidadian Horace Ové. It was his first film and he eventually became one of Britain's top filmmakers, photographers and artists. In Baldwin's off-the-cuff speech at the WISC he explained how he came to be called Baldwin, as his ancestors belonged to a white man with that name, "*Baldwin's N* became the title of the film." Baldwin also discussed topics familiar on both sides of the Atlantic, like rich and powerful white countries bombing poor Black and Brown countries:

> "We know, no matter what the professions of my happy country may be, that we are not bombing people out of existence in the name of freedom. If it were freedom we were concerned about, then long, long ago we would've done something about Johannesburg, South Africa. And if we were concerned with freedom, boys and girls would not, as I stand here, be perishing in the streets of Harlem. We are concerned with power. Nothing more than that. And most unlucky for the Western World, it has consolidated its power on the backs of people who are now going to die rather than be used any longer."

Until the 1970s, WISC was a meeting place for activists such as Guyanese couple Eric and Jessica Huntley, Trinidadian John La Rose and Jamaican Connie Mark, who between them, pioneered bookshops, publishing houses, Saturday schools and educational resources such as a mobile exhibition on the Black presence in World War II and Mary Seacole.

In 1981, the Brixton uprisings (often referred to as riots by the mainstream press), which took place in the Borough of Lambeth, south London, sparked unrest in other towns and cities across the country caused by the racism inherent in the system. It was apparent that radical change was needed in British society. Activists in east London in the Borough of Hackney, such as Jamaican, Lloyd King and the Hackney Ethnic Minorities Library Consultative Committee, lobbied, protested, and campaigned to get libraries to stock Black history books and remove the racist literature on display – books like *Tarzan* and *Tintin*. They even organised a 'sit-in' in Hackney Town Hall and refused to leave until the council took action. The group also campaigned to appoint Black librarians as there were none at the time.

A London-wide anti-racism campaign had been launched in 1984; London Against Racism Year was championed by Ken Livingstone, head of the Greater London Council. Local campaigns and activism intensified and continued post-1984. In 1985, Hackney Council pledged a year of Anti-Racism, rooted in grassroots activism. Therefore, Baldwin's 1985 visit came amidst this intense British civil rights era and supported local anti-racist activists. The Hackney protesters had already won a fight to rename Dalston Lane Library after the revolutionary, Trinidadian intellectual, C.L.R. James. James was the author of *The Black Jacobins,* a groundbreaking work about the Haitian Revolution and an original member of the League of Coloured Peoples, the 1930s Black British Civil Rights group.

Hackney was at the centre of racial change in the 1980s. In 1984, the Commission for Racial Equality found that Hackney Council was racist in its allocation of housing. Black people either could not get council housing at all, or they were given the worst houses in the worst areas with the most repairs needed. They received the least support, as well as suffering random physical racist attacks. The violent white supremacist group, the National Front, sold its hate magazine *Spearhead* in Brick Lane in Tower Hamlets, a neighbouring borough of Hackney. Their publications would state that "black people ate dirt and faeces and that all black people should be stripped of citizenship and deported within ten years." The National Front were known to attack Black people for no reason other than their skin colour.

In 1978, Black teenager Michael Ferreira was just one of several people murdered in unprovoked attacks by men chanting racist slogans. The police, who were supposed to protect the community, were constantly involved in the deaths of young Black men in their custody. In 1983, Colin Roach died in suspicious circumstances in Stoke Newington police station. The police stated he walked into the station with a shotgun and fired it into his mouth. His family, and the Black community in general, never believed that story and campaigned tirelessly for justice. This was the backdrop to Baldwin's visit to an inner London borough which resembled where he was born and grew up in Harlem.

Another grassroots organisation fighting against racist institutions was the volunteer-run Hackney Community Defence Association (HCDA). They were extremely active in the fight against police corruption and brutality, achieving a high level of success with limited resources. This grassroots, self-funded group, investigated police officers, took statements from police victims and submitted evidence to the Home Office about serious and widespread police corruption in the 1980s. It was not until 1992 that officers at Stoke Newington police station (nicknamed Coke Newington) were brought to public notice. In 1995 up to 45 Hackney officers were investigated for selling and/or distributing drugs (including cocaine) in the borough, while at the same time arresting innocent Black people for drugs offences. The case attracted constant widespread media attention throughout 1992, and as Graham Smith, one of the founders of the HCDA who did a PhD on the scandal said, "after two years, it disappeared without a trace."

Despite this background of tension and struggle, Baldwin was comfortable visiting the CLR James Library and meeting fellow activists in the fight against racism. Baldwin was able to endorse their fight for civil rights and amplify the hope of the local Black community that change would come. His words were powerful in raising awareness that collectively, it was possible to effect change and bring about a more equitable society.

"Not everything that is faced can be changed, but nothing can be changed until it is faced."

– James Baldwin, *No Name in the Street*

On 17th May, 2024, Black History Walks, in collaboration with Nubian Jak, installed a blue plaque to honour Baldwin's visit at the original site of the CLR James Library on Dalston Lane. Now renamed the Adiaha Antigha Centre, the building is home to Hackney Volunteer Services and is only 100 metres away from the site of the iconic Four Aces reggae club, which was torn down despite a residents' campaign protesting to  save it. The plaque does not only honour James Baldwin but reflects and respects the work of people like Lloyd King, Dan Thea, Mackenzie Frank, Leila Hassan Howe, Margaret Busby and the many other Black British civil rights activists.

References
1. Mike Watson, CLR James Library and its history https://lrgr14. wordpress.com/2014/07/25/the-local-importance-of-c-l-r-james-and-dalston-library/#:~:text=In%201985%20the%20Dalston%20 Library,'Anti%2DRacist%20Year' 2014.
2. *Baldwin's Nigger*, film directed by Horace Ové, 1969
3. Gaverne Bennett and Christian Hogsberg, *Celebrating CLR James in Hackney* Redwords, 2015.
4. *Baldwin's Nigger* full transcript https://whileseated.medium. com/baldwins-nigger-transcription-of-james-baldwin-in-london-1968-358f27723506
5. *Baldwin's Nigger* edited transcript https://blacklikevanilla. com/baldwins-nigger-a-1969-conversation-with-james-baldwin-and-dick-gregory/
6. Operation Jackpot, corrupt cops in Hackney https://www. independent.co.uk/news/uk/police-could-face-criminal-charges-after-drugs-inquiry-officers-in-northeast-london-alleged-to-have-sold-cocaine-and-planted-evidence-1391845.html
7. Trevor Monerville and Tunay Hassan, 'Radical history of Hackney' https://hackneyhistory.wordpress.com/hcda/fight-ing-the-lawmen/
8. 'Who killed Michael Ferreira?' https://hackneyhistory.word-press.com/2022/01/06/who-killed-michael-ferreira-part-one/
9. 'Blazing a trail for Black British writing, Jacaranda books' https://blogs.bl.uk/english-and-drama/2020/07/blazing-a-trail-for-black-british-writing-jacarandas-twenty-in-2020.html

James Baldwin, December 1984, Amsterdam.
Photo: Anefo/Dutch National Archives

About the Authors

Rashidah Ismaili AbuBakr writes plays, poetry, fiction, and cultural critiques. She teaches on the Creative Writing Low Residence progamme at Wilkes University, USA. Her work has been widely anthologised, most recently including a short story in *New Daughters of Africa* (2020), a poem in *Afrika im Gedicht* a multimedia exhibition in Zurich, (2022), and *Bessie* a play performed at (HIFA), Harare International Festival of Arts in Zimbabwe, 2018. Her first book of fiction is a trilogy: *An African Woman in New York,* 2016. She has been active in literary and cultural movements including Umbra, the Black Arts Movement and Black Creators for Black Children. She remains active in African Literature Association, Associated Writers Programme, PEN and Pen & Brush. She is an advocate for human rights and literacy for young people with an emphasis on females in Africa and the African Diaspora. She has hosted Salon d'Afrique, an international gathering of artists and cultural workers at her home in Harlem for over forty years.

Victor Adebowale is a respected entrepreneur, coach, thought leader and writer. With a passion for enhancing community access to vital services, he has significantly impacted various sectors through his visionary leadership and unwavering commitment to social justice. He is the founder and Chair of the social consultancy Collaborate CIC and Visionable, a ground-breaking health technology company. He serves as a non-executive Director of the Co-Operative Group and is the Chair of Social Enterprise UK and the NHS Confederation. His exceptional service to the unemployed and homeless earned him a CBE, and in 2001, he was appointed a crossbench peer.

Victor is also the recipient of multiple honorary doctorates and often appears on radio and television featuring on popular programmes including BBC's *Question Time* and Radio 4's *Desert Island Discs.*

Toyin Agbetu is a scholar-activist and lecturer of anthropology at University College London. He uses a decolonial lens to teach about racialisation, ethnicity and nationalism. As a researcher,

About the Authors

Toyin works on digital rights alongside reparatory and social justice projects tackling institutional racism, structural violence and algorithmic discrimination. He is an award-winning filmmaker and a passionate advocate for fusing education with countercultural art forms to build a just and equitable human rights centred world.

Prior to his academic career, Toyin made a mark in the 1980s' music scene with numerous record releases and created the 'streetsoul' genre in the UK. Toyin also founded Ligali, a Pan-African organisation that, since 2001, has been challenging Afriphobia and the misrepresentation of African people, history, and culture in the media, public spaces and social services. He is a community educator with the IDPAD (International Decade for People of African Descent 2015-2024) Empowerment Centre in Hackney.

Rosanna Amaka is a writer from London. The human condition and the effects/impact of Black history are features in her work. Her debut novel *The Book of Echoes*, was shortlisted for the Authors's Club First Novel Award, the RSL Christopher Bland Prize and the HWA Debut Crown Award. Her second novel *Rose and the Burma Sky* was inspired by a conversation with her grandmother and follows the journey of an African soldier fighting in WWII.

Michelle Yaa Asantewa is an award-winning author, independent educator, cultural consultant and publisher. Her publications include the young adult novel, *Elijah, The Awakening and Other Poems, Guyanese Komfa: The Ritual Art of Trance* and *Something Buried in the Yard,* published by Way Wive Wordz Publishing, which she co-founded in 2014. She is the editor of the anthology *In Search of Mami Wata*, which centres on African and Caribbean water spirits. *Mama Lou Tales*, a biography of her mother Lucille Davis received a prize from the Guyana Literary Prize in 2022. Michelle is the course leader on The Amazing James Baldwin, African Women Resistance Leaders: Spiritual and Political and Afrofuturism Creative Writing short courses. She co-facilitates the Toni-Morrison: Her Life Her Work and Andrea Levy courses. Her first collection of short stories, *The Geometry Set and the Mami Wata, Children's Activity Book* will be published in the autumn of 2024.

Eugen Bacon is an African Australian author of several novels and collections. She's a British Fantasy Award winner, a Foreword Indies Award winner, a twice World Fantasy Award finalist, and a finalist in other awards. Eugen was announced in the honour list of the Otherwise Fellowships for "doing exciting work in gender and speculative fiction." *Danged Black Thing* made the Otherwise Award Honour List as a "sharp collection of Afro-Surrealist work," and was a 2024 Philip K. Dick Award nominee. Eugen's creative work has appeared worldwide, including in *Apex Magazine, Award Winning Australian Writing, Fantasy, Fantasy & Science Fiction*, and *Year's Best African Speculative Fiction*. Visit her at eugenbacon.com

Lindsay Barrett is a Jamaican-born writer who has written, published and produced in all genres. He is also a photographer, journalist and broadcaster. His acclaimed debut novel, *Song for Mumu* was published by Longman (1967). He was winner of the Conrad Kent Rivers Memorial Award (1970).

When he left Jamaica at the age of nineteen, he travelled extensively around Europe, USA, North Africa and West Africa before finally settling in Nigeria. During this period he lived and worked in some of these countries, writing at the same time.

Between the 1960s and the 1980s Lindsay was involved with Black literary and creative movements and groups across the diaspora and on the continent including the Mbari Artists Club in Ibadan, the Caribbean Artists movement in London and the Black Arts movement in the USA. He participated in historic productions such as World Festival of Black Arts in Senegal and at Keskidee Arts Centre in London.

In 2017, he received a Lifetime Achievement Award "for excellence in creative writing" by the Institute of Arts and Culture at the University of Port Harcourt.

Gabriella Beckles-Raymond, Senior Fellow (HEA), is an independent interdisciplinary philosopher, writer, educator, wife, mother, sister, friend, basketball coach, and Co-CEO of EQBR. Her work has been published internationally in a range of journals, books and commissioned reports. Gabriella's research and writing is concerned with questions of love, moral psychology, culture, justice and ethics and what it means to 'Liv Good' at the intersections of systemic domination. She has over twenty years of experience in education as a leader, administrator, faculty member, and program developer. She is the founder of the Liv Good Collective Knowledge Production group, a member of Metronomes Steel Orchestra, the Collegium of Black Women Philosophers, and the Caribbean Philosophical Association.

Alan Bell currently heads BLK, a company specializing in graphic design for community-based organizations that serve the health, educational and social needs of inner-city communities. He was editor and publisher of *Gaysweek,* New York's first LGBTQ weekly newspaper and the first owned by an African American; editor of *Kujisource,* a Black AIDS newsletter; and editor and publisher of several magazines for the Black LGBTQ community, most notably the monthly newsmagazine, *BLK*. Alan was a typesetting production manager before founding Black Jack, a safer sex club for Black gay men, whose *Black Jack Newsletter* eventually led to *BLK*. Published from 1988 until 1994, *BLK* won numerous awards and is part of the permanent collection of the National Museum of African American History and Culture. For six years, he was film critic for the *Los Angeles Sentinel,* a mainstream Black weekly.

Bell holds BA and MA degrees in Sociology, and a BS degree in Business.

Selina Brown is an author, marketing consultant and event producer. Raised by her British mother and Jamaican granny, Selina was an avid reader from a young age. At 16, she became the Youth MP for Nottingham, her love for words gained her two Degrees and a Masters at 21 years old. After living and working in New York, Jamaica, Kenya and Gambia, Selina founded Little Miss Creative, an award-winning Female Development Agency that empowers girls in schools across the UK. During the pandemic she wrote the picture book series *Nena* that became popular in 2020. The same year Selina launched the internationally renowned Black British Book Festival, which aims to celebrate new and emerging Black British authors across all genres of literature.

Michael Campbell is a Black British writer, visual artist and teacher of art. Michael was born to a Jamaican mother and father and is currently based in Essex.

Encounters with James Baldwin

Michael's poetry often examines the individual, the familial, and the societal. He is on the lookout for everyday moments of virtue and is especially interested in faith and how it can reform or even transform a person's lived experience. Michael teaches art at secondary school level and sees art as one of the oldest human projects that stretches back to the palaeolithic era.

Michael's poems 'Secret Place' and 'Maroon' were included in the Inscribe anthology *Filigree,* which was edited by Nii Ayikwei Parkes and Kadija George Sesay. He has performed at Kings College London and the Barbican Library.

Fred D'Aguiar is a British-Guyanese writer of poetry, fiction, drama and essays. Born in London of Guyanese parents, he grew up in Guyana and returned to London for his secondary and tertiary education. His memoir, *Year of Plagues* (Carcanet), was published in 2021. His most recent poetry book, his eighth, is *For the Unnamed* (Carcanet, 2023). His sixth novel, *Children of Paradise* (Granta, 2016), is about Jonestown, Guyana. He is Professor of English at UCLA.

Thomas Glave is the author of four books and the editor of *Our Caribbean: A Gathering of Lesbian and Gay Writing from the Antilles.* A two-time Fulbright Scholar and honorary visiting professor at the University of Liverpool, he serves on the editorial boards of *Transition,* Outhistory.org, and *Wasafiri.* He is a trustee of Writing West Midlands and Peepal Tree Press.

Sonia Grant is an independent historian and scholar, non-fiction writer, archival researcher and photographic exhibition curator. Her main areas of interest revolve around the exploration of themes encompassing "hidden histories, untold stories and marginalised voices", with work being published in *Huffington Post* and *BBC History Revealed,* among others.

Currently, she is writing a biography on Charlotta Bass, the first woman of colour to run as a vice-presidential candidate in the 1952 US election, and a book chronicling the settlement of WWI civilian internees, men of colour repatriated from Germany to Britain who, she argues, were the precursor of so-called multicultural Britain decades before the arrival of *HMT Empire Windrush.*

About the Authors

Zita Holbourne is a multi-award-winning author and multi-disciplinary artist, campaigner and activist. In her creative practice she works as a writer, performance poet, visual artist, vocalist and educator. She is a community activist, equality and human rights campaigner and trade union leader, co-founder of Black Activists Rising Against Cuts (BARAC) UK and joint National Chair of Artists' Union England.

She is the author of *Striving for Equality, Freedom and Justice* (Hansib, 2017) and co-author of *Roots and Rebellion* (JK Publishers, 2024) and has contributed to over forty books as a writer, poet and illustrator, including *New Daughters of Africa.* She is a guest editor, mentor and facilitator for *Writing Our Legacy.*

Zita is the winner of the Jessica Kingsley Writing Prize 2023. She has worked globally as a performance poet, exhibiting artist and public speaker.

Paterson Joseph is a beloved British actor and writer. Recently seen on *Vigil, Noughts + Crosses* and *Boat Story*, he has also starred in *The Leftovers, Timeless, Law & Order UK* and *Peep Show*. He plays Arthur Slugworth in the *Wonka* movie. Paterson won the Royal Society of Literature's Christopher Bland Prize and the Historical Writers' Association's 2023 Debut Historical Crown Award for his debut novel *The Secret Diaries of Charles Ignatius Sancho.*

Peter Kalu's short stories range in style from the realist to the surreal to the carnivalesque and can be found in anthologies including *Collision* (Comma Press, 2023), *Glimpse* (Peepal Tree, 2023), *Lancashire Stories* (Lancashire Libraries, 2023), *Closure* (Peepal Tree, 2015), *Seaside Special* (Bluemoose, 2018) and *A Country To Call Home* (Unbound, 2017). His alternative reality novel *One Drop* (Andersen Press) was published in 2022. He was part of a team that created the story architecture for the RPG game *Simulacrum Funk*. He writes occasional book and art reviews that can be found at www.peterkalu.com

Roy McFarlane is a poet, playwright and former Youth and Community worker born in Birmingham of Jamaican parentage, living in Brighton. He is currently a Poetry Book Society collection selector and the National Canal Laureate.

Encounters with James Baldwin

The former Birmingham Poet Laureate has co-edited *Celebrate Wha? Ten Black British Poets from the Midlands* (Smokestack). His three collections are published by Nine Arches Press: *Beginning With Your Last Breath;* and *The Healing Next Time* (shortlisted for the Ted Hughes Award and longlisted for the Jhalak Prize). His greatly anticipated third collection *Living by Troubled Waters* was published in 2022.

He's performed nationally and internationally sharing his passion for social justice, equality, identity love and the healing power of poetry as a witness to our times.

Ronnie McGrath is a Black neo-surrealist writer, poet, and visual artist. He is a founding member of the cultural musical group The London Afro Blok, which toured Europe and opened the Commonwealth Games in Canada. A former Creative Writing lecturer at London College of Communications, he is an associate lecturer of Creative Writing at Imperial College London and Bath Spa University. In his role as a community artist, Ronnie uses creative writing as a therapeutic tool to work with members of the unhoused community, and people who suffer from chronic pain, anxiety, and poor mental health. Ronnie's published works include visual art in *Callaloo,* a journal of African American Arts and Letters; *Data Trace*, a full collection of his postmodern poetry; 'Contraband', a short story in *Glimpse*, an anthology of Black speculative fiction; 'Flatline', in the anthology *Black Lives Have Always Mattered;* and 'Megan's Sparkle', in *Filigree, Contemporary Black British Poetry.*

Michael McMillan, Arts.D. is a London-based writer, playwright, artist/curator and scholar, best known for *The Front Room* installation, iterated in the Netherlands, Curacao, Johannesburg, France and recently, Toronto, as part of Tate Britain's *Life Between Islands* (2023–24). It is the basis of the BBC4 documentary *Tales from the Front Room* (2007) and his revised edition *The Front Room: Diaspora Migrant Aesthetics in the Home* (Lund Humphries, 2023) and is permanently displayed at the Museum of the Home, where his performance piece that he wrote and directed after 2019, *Waiting for myself to appear* is a triptych film installation.

About the Authors

Recent writing includes: *Sonic Vibrations: Sound systems, lovers rock and dub* for WritersMosaic. His recent installation *I Miss My Mum's Cookin'* was nominated for a Brighton Fringe award (2023). His Arts Doctorate is from Middlesex University (2010), and he is currently Associate Lecturer in Cultural & Historical Studies at London College of Fashion (UAL), and VIAD Research Associate at University of Johannesburg.

Tony Medina was born in the South Bronx and raised in the Throg's Neck Housing Projects. A United States Army veteran, he holds a master's and PhD from Binghamton University, SUNY, and is Howard University's first professor of Creative Writing. Tony is a multi-genre author/editor of 25 award-winning books for adults and young people. His work appears in more than 160 anthologies and journals, including 'Seven Steps to Heaven Haiku', featured in the Academy of American Poets' *Poem-a-Day*. Among Tony's many titles are the Black Lives Matter anthology, *Resisting Arrest: Poems to Stretch the Sky; Death, With Occasional Smiling* (poetry); *Thirteen Ways of Looking at a Black Boy* (children's), *I Am Alfonso Jones* (graphic novel), *Che Che Colé* (fiction); the poetry collection, *Because the Sky* (Sable Books); two Third World Press titles: *Serious Trouble* (poetry) and *Everywhere Drums: Poets from the Black Arts to Black Lives Matter* (co-edited with Mudiwa Pettus); as well as a hybrid collection of poetry and fiction, *Rock the Bells: For Hip Hop @ 50*.

Bill V. Mullen is Professor Emeritus of American Studies at Purdue University. He is the author of *James Baldwin: Living in Fire* (Pluto Press, 2019, 2024). He is co-author with Jeanelle Hope of *The Black Antifascist Tradition: Fighting Back from Anti-Lynching to Abolition* (Haymarket Books, 2024). He is a member of the organizing collective for the United States Campaign for Academic and Cultural Boycott of Israel (USACBI).

Nducu wa Ngugi is a prize-winning author. He holds a BA in Black Studies from Oberlin College, Ohio, an M.Ed., and an Ed.S in Teacher Leadership from Mercer University, Atlanta, Georgia. He is the author of *City Murders*, a novel published by the East African Educational Publishers. *City Murders* was short-listed for the Jomo Kenyatta Prize for Literature (2015). His second novel, *The Dead Came Calling*, was published by EAEP in 2018. His third novel, *Benji's Big Win*, won the Jomo Kenyatta Prize in 2022. A sequel, *Benji's Mountain Adventures*, is slated for release by EAEP 2024.

Nducu is the Chief Executive Officer of the Ngugi wa Thiong'o Foundation. He lives on Long Island, New York, with his wife, Grace Nyambura, and daughter, Nyambura wa Nducu.

Lola Oh is a Black British poet, photographer and facilitator. Lola was born to a Jamaican mother and a Nigerian father, and is currently based in South London. Through her poetry, Lola uses her work to explore family, loss, and ideas of Black womanhood. Through photography, Lola uses her creative eye to document the world around her, distilling the essence of human emotions in the mundane, or intimate moments of everyday life. Lola's poem 'Bad Daughters' was shortlisted for *The White Review's* Poetry Prize. Lola is an alumni of the Roundhouse Poetry Collective, Griots Well and Barbican Young Poets. She is a Roundhouse Slam Finalist, and has been featured by Apples and Snakes, BBC1xtra, English Touring Theatre, and Roundhouse's The Last Word Festival.

Ewuare X. Osayande is a lawyer, independent scholar, poet, essayist and the author of many books including *Blood Luxury* with an introduction by Amiri Baraka and *Black Phoenix Uprising*. His latest book is titled *Our Breath is the Whisper of Our Ancestors' Defiance: The Poetry Anthology* (1993–2023). His work has been included in a number of anthologies including the critically acclaimed *Black Fire This Time,* Vols. I and II. A former professor of African American Studies at Rutgers University, he is the founding editor of *The Poetariat*, an international social justice poetry journal. Ewuare is the 2024 recipient of the Richard H. Semsker Prize in Civil Rights Law. Osayande.org

Nii Ayikwei Parkes is a Ghanaian writer, editor and publisher. His début novel, *Tail of the Blue Bird,* was shortlisted for the Commonwealth Prize and won France's two major prizes for translated fiction – Prix Baudelaire and Prix Laure-Bataillon – in 2014. Translated in multiple languages, he has also written for *National Geographic, Financial Times, The Guardian,* and *Lonely Planet,* and been the recipient of residencies and fellowships from the Hutchins Center for African and African American Research at Harvard University, the University of Southampton, the Civitella

About the Authors

Ranieri Foundation, the V&A Museum and the California State University, Los Angeles. A 2007 laureate of Ghana's national ACRAG award for literary advocacy, Nii Ayikwei serves on the boards of World Literature Today and the Caine Prize. His most recent books are *The Geez*, a collection of poems, *The Ga Picture Alphabet,* a children's book and *Azúcar,* a novel.

Anton Phillips has produced some notable successes, including Trevor Rhone's *Two Can Play,* at the Arts Theatre, and at the Theatre Royal, Stratford; *Remembrance,* by Derek Walcott at The Tricycle Theatre; and *Sitting in Limbo* by Judy Hepburn and Dawn Penso, which toured to the Caribbean. His most notable achievement was to produce and direct *The Amen Corner,* by James Baldwin, at The Tricycle and the Lyric Theatre, Shaftesbury Avenue, London. He has also directed in Germany, Holland, and at the National Theatre of Ghana and has been a theatre consultant to the British Council in Tanzania.

Ray Shell has been a permanent fixture in the West End since 1978 when he starred in Oscar Johnson and Lon Satton's *Little Willie Jr's Ressurection.* He has starred in productions such as *Starlight Express, Miss Saigon, The Lion King* and *The Body Guard.*

He is also the author of *Iced, Carolina Red, Spike Lee: The Eternal Maverick* and the BBC Radio 3 drama *Jubilee* with Garth Bardsley. Ray has his own imprint: Street Angels Books at www.streetangelsbooks.co.uk

SuAndi is a proactive creator, using the arts as a vehicle for learning and understanding across diverse communities. She is a recognised international performance artist and an in-demand conference speaker. SuAndi pushes at the boundaries of poetry, to writing narratives for exhibitions, short films, community plays, the Mary Seacole libretto and oral history research projects. Her one-woman show *The Story of M* is now on the A-Level syllabus. A curator of visual arts, a producer and a director of community-based performances in partnership with National Black Arts Alliance members, she is acknowledged for raising the profile of regional Black artists as NBAA's freelance Cultural Director since 1985.

In 1999 she received an OBE, followed by Lancaster University and Manchester Metropolitan University honorary degrees, the

BME Network 'Inspirational Award', in 2023 Manchester's Culture Special Recognition Awards and is a Writing Fellow at Leicester University. In 2024, she received the Benson Medal and was made an Honorary Fellow by the Royal Society of Literature.

Tade Thompson is a multi-award winning writer of novels, short stories, and screenplays. His background is in medicine, psychiatry, and social anthropology. He is a winner of the Arthur C. Clarke award for his book *Rosewater.* He is a fellow of the Royal Society of Literature and the Vice President of the British Science Fiction Association. He lives and works on the south coast of England.

Patrick Vernon is a sought-after broadcaster, public speaker, and EDI adviser. He writes blogs and articles for the national and international media on healthcare, cultural heritage and race. In 2020 Patrick was selected by British *Vogue* as one of Britain's top twenty campaigners and since then he has been included in the Powerlist of 100 Influential Black People in Britain. In 2020 Patrick co-authored *100 Great Black Britons* based on his campaign. In 2004 he also co-authored an anthology, *Black Grief.*

Tony Warner is the author of *Black History Walks Volume 1,* the first book on the Black history of London's streets. The book is published by the award-winning, Black female-owned and run Jacaranda Books.

He is also co-author on the Pearson GCSE History exam textbook which is partly based on his Notting Hill walking tour. It features the fight for Black British civil rights in the 1950s–1970s. The book is presently used in 140 schools by 10,000 pupils.

www.blackhistorywalks.co.uk

James Baldwin, 1985

"Know from whence you came. If you know whence you came, there are absolutely no limitations to where you can go."

– James Baldwin

More diverse books to read and enjoy

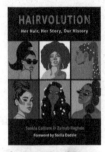

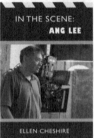

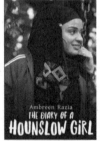

www.aurorametro.com